BLURRED
LINES

Can detective Miller solve the mystery of a
murder and a kidnapping?

DIANE M DICKSON

Paperback published by The Book Folks

London, 2020

© Diane Dickson

ISBN 979-8-6588-4011-6

www.thebookfolks.com

This one is for my dad, who taught me to love books.

Prologue

It was raining. Carol tried to focus on the cool dampness instead of the fire in her gut. She couldn't feel her legs and now her arms were tingling, her fingers were numb. But the moisture on her face was a kiss from the heavens. She tried to push herself nearer to the tree. The beautiful big cherry; focus point of the garden. Perhaps she could lean against it. But her legs wouldn't work, and she didn't have any upper body strength. Arthritis had been slowly taking it away for a few years, but now, with this, the last of it was gone. She sobbed. A strange strangled sound. It wasn't helping but was impossible to stop. The previous calls for help had brought no-one and left her without the strength to try again.

She moved a hand to the middle of her stomach. Pressure, that was what she needed, pressure on the wound. The pain was indescribable. The warm wet slime terrified her. She knew it was blood, though in the gloom she couldn't see. It wasn't pumping, though. That was good, wasn't it? If it wasn't pumping, then there were no arteries damaged. Her shoulders were agony. Didn't it mean something. Something about blood in her abdomen, well of course. An owl cried in the distance. She had always loved the owls. Shivering came in great spasms, but she didn't feel cold anymore. She felt calmer, she was tired – so very tired. There was a buzzing inside her head. The edges of her vision were darkening, moving in, taking what little light there was. She turned to look towards the house. The kitchen window was filled by a warm glow, it made her weep.

So, this was what it had come to. All the fear and the worry and desperate attempts to change things. It had all come to this and she might as well let go now. Nobody was coming to help. Even the boys had gone. She had heard them; one of them had been crying. She had just a moment to feel sorry about it all and then – she let go.

Chapter 1

Tanya Miller didn't hear the chime of her phone. The sound was drowned by the rush of water. She had the shower turned to high and the temperature hot enough to colour her shoulders and upper arms bright pink. The bathroom was fogged with steam. After a fierce workout in her dressing room, using the home gym she had paid too much for and didn't have the chance to use often enough, the pound of water on her screaming muscles was bliss. With a sigh, she stepped out and reached for one of her huge fluffy bath sheets. It was the last day before she went back to work. The investigation into her conduct during the last case was over. She had been cautioned, but the worst possibility, loss of rank, had not happened. There would be a black mark on her record and that hurt. She was aiming for the top in the police service and didn't need any negatives. But it was what it was and the only thing to do now was to get back to work. She was looking forward to it but intended to enjoy this last day, the worry gone, replaced by anticipation and excitement.

Then she noticed the missed call light blinking on the device and knew even before she strode across the bedroom that when she read the message on her mobile, this final day of leave would be over.

She could have left it until she'd had the croissants and coffee waiting for her in the kitchen. But there were three missed calls, all from the dispatcher and one from DC Lewis, so she didn't, and within a half an hour was in her car battling the early morning traffic. The coffee was in her go-cup and the croissants dropping greasy flakes onto her new black trousers as she drove.

DC Kate Lewis would meet her at the crime scene, a detached house in Summertown, an affluent area on the outskirts of the city. Efficient as always, she had already begun to mobilise the team. She'd arranged for an operational name to be generated, Songbird, and was now filling Tanya in on the few facts they had.

"DS Harris is on his way into headquarters, boss. He's going to set up the room. I live near, so it made sense for me to come straight over. DC Price has been told but he's away until tomorrow and DC Rollinson has been informed."

"Her transfer hasn't come through, then?"

"No, boss. I did hear she is having second thoughts. She asked for a meeting with HR. If she goes to Yorkshire it obviously means leaving her family and now it's come to the crunch, I reckon she's getting cold feet."

"I'll have to find time to have a chat with her. We'll be short on bodies anyway with DI Finch gone."

"Yes, boss."

"Anyway, that can all wait. For now, tell me what we know."

"A triple nine call this morning. Next-door neighbour looking out of her bedroom window saw the victim, Carol Barker, lying on the grass. She called the ambulance service which generated an alert for us. The paramedics attended but knew pretty quickly the best thing they could do was simply stand by and wait. Local patrol officers have secured the location, and scene of crime team and the coroner's people are on the way."

"I'll be with you in about" – Tanya glanced at the sat nav – "twenty minutes if the traffic doesn't get any worse."

* * *

The house was one of a short terrace of Victorian villas. Bay windows, decorative curved porches over the door, red brick under a tiled apex roof. The small area at the front had been turned into parking for a black Fiesta, not new but well kept. There was already crime scene tape stretched along the low wall and a uniformed officer stationed in front of the gate. Tanya flashed her warrant card and he noted her name on his clipboard as he stepped aside.

"Crime Scene are in the back garden, ma'am. You can go down that alley." He pointed to a narrow space between the buildings. "There are scene suits in the box over there." There was a white van with the back door standing open, near to where Tanya had parked. She slid into the paper coveralls and pulled elasticated bootees over her shoes.

At the back of the property, the garden was long and narrow. The lawn was surrounded by flower borders, still winter-bare with fleece protecting a couple of shrubs. The centre of the grass was patchy, mostly due to the roots of the big tree which was two-thirds of the way down the garden towards the rear fence. Someone had built a low bench around a half of the trunk and sprawled across the ground, her head partly under the wooden seat, was the body of a woman dressed in nightclothes. The front of the pale nightie was darkened by a stiffening patch of blood and more of it soaked the grass of the lawn.

Tanya didn't walk along the safe route that had been marked out by plastic steppingstones, but she raised her hands in greeting to Dave Chance who stood at the far side of the corpse making notes on a tablet computer.

Already there were small plastic evidence tents around the lawn and the blue scene cover was being erected. The pale body was unreal and wraithlike against the green of the grass and the patches of blood dark in the pale light of the cloudy morning.

Dave Chance walked towards her. "Morning, Tanya. This is nasty." He nodded towards the tent which now protected and hid the body. "There's blood across the grass, looks as though it has tracked all the way from the house. I've got people in there now."

"So, she came outside herself?"

"Looks to me as though she staggered out here, maybe running away, maybe trying to get help. There are footprints on the path and the grass. Her feet are filthy. She is wet through. I reckon she's been out here a while; it was raining last night, her hair and face are soaked. Dr Hewitt is on his way."

"Okay. Thanks, Dave. Have you seen DC Lewis?"

"Yes, she's over by the house."

"I'll have a word with her. When Dr Hewitt arrives, will you have someone come and fetch me."

"I will. You're looking well, Tanya."

"Yes, well, enforced rest. I had a chance to catch up on my sleep, didn't I? I was bored to death though. It's good to be back. Well, not good for this poor woman but…" She shrugged her shoulders. The scene of crime officer nodded, and she could tell by the way the skin around his eyes crinkled that he was smiling at her behind his mask.

"You might as well get under the back porch for now," he said. "I reckon it's going to start raining again. Nothing for you to do here for the moment and you don't want your hairdo spoiled, do you?" He raised a finger to point at her ponytail still damp from the shower.

Tanya raised her eyebrows at him and shook her head.

Kate Lewis stood beside the back door under a wooden porch. She turned as Tanya climbed the two narrow steps to stand beside her. "Blood there across the kitchen floor, boss, and it looks as though it's all the way down the hallway. Crime scene bods are inside the living room right now."

She turned her tablet so Tanya could watch the images streaming from a headcam being worn by one of the officers. "There's blood in there, it's spread around a fair bit. There's a bit of disturbance of the furniture, cushions on the floor and what have you. It looks as though the assault happened indoors and then, for some reason, she came outside."

"That's cool." Tanya pointed to the screen.

"Yes, we began trialling it while you were on leave."

"Oh, I want one. Okay. We need to organise house-to-house enquiries as soon as we can. It's…" Tanya glanced at her watch "…half past eight. I suppose we'll have missed some of the locals who are out at work already, but we'll catch who we can. We'll get some of the uniforms on it. Go back to the office and have a quick briefing with the team and then get stuck in. Where is the neighbour who called the ambulance?"

"Back in her own house. She was pretty shaken up. There's an officer with her. She's a… Mrs Cartwright."

"Okay, that's where I'll go first. Can you organise preliminaries with the officers we have here? It'll be a start anyway. Afterwards, you might be best off going back and supervising the rest of the setting up. I know Sergeant Harris has made a start but let's be honest – he's not as good at the computer stuff as you are. You do the detail better." She was rewarded by a grin from the other woman.

"Okay, no problem, I'll just go and speak to the sergeant."

They walked together to the road where a few neighbours had begun to cluster in gateways. Children passing on the way to school gaped and giggled at the sight of the officers in protective gear.

"Can we tape off this end of the road, officer?" Tanya said. "And further down by the junction. Apologise to the neighbours for the inconvenience, but we can do without all the ghouls and there are plenty of other routes for them to follow."

Kate re-joined her and they watched as the crowd were pushed back and cars drawn across the roadway. The medical examiner's car arrived followed by a van with the logo of the local radio station.

The circus proper was underway.

"Here we go then." Tanya sighed. "It didn't take them long to hear about it. Right, let's get on." Kate turned to walk past the roadblock to her own car.

"Oh, before you go – I've got this," Tanya said. She moved around to the rear of her car which was parked beside the gate and dragged out a cardboard box and a plastic carrier. "Perhaps you could get it set up."

Kate peered into the white bag and grinned when she saw the two packets of ground coffee, one decaffeinated. "Is this for your office, boss?"

"Nah, let's put it in the incident room. Time we had a bit of style, don't you think?" Tanya was smiling as Kate drove away. Okay, she couldn't really afford it, and she still didn't fully understand the instinct that had made her splash out on the coffee maker but, with Finch gone, taking his all-singing, all-dancing machine with him, it had amused her and, when all was said and done, the coffee from the machine in the hallway was pretty much undrinkable. It wasn't practical to be forever nipping out to the local Costa. The grin on Kate Lewis's face had been worth the money.

Back in the garden, as she approached the plastic shelter Tanya felt a flicker of excitement. She was saddened for the woman whose body had lain for hours in the rain, but she would work for her and she would get justice. It was all that could be done now. Despite the circumstances, it felt good to be back.

Chapter 2

It was too soon for Simon Hewitt to give her any meaningful information, but Tanya walked across to say hello. He leaned towards her and for a moment, she thought he might hug her. She took a half step back and he straightened.

"Good to see you, Tanya. I meant to call you while you were on leave. But, well you know how it is, time just gets away, doesn't it? I hear the inquiry went your way."

"Sort of. I do understand that I should have waited for back up instead of acting alone. But sometimes you just have to get on with it. I knew people were in danger and I didn't see I had any other option. I suppose if that poor girl hadn't died, they would have been more understanding. They didn't throw me out, anyway. I have to accept their ruling, but it still rankles."

"I'll bet. Not to worry. I guess the only thing is to put it behind you. Listen, I was wondering if, now you're back, maybe we could meet up for a coffee or something? Just for a chat, you know."

The bit of his face visible between the hair cover and the mask flushed and Tanya felt sorry for him. He was so very talented, among the best in his field she had heard it said, and yet he was shy and diffident in his dealings with her. She never heard of any friends, no partner, and he never mentioned family. For her it would be bliss, but she knew it wasn't that way for most people.

"Okay. Yes, sounds nice." She turned away and screwed her eyes closed. That had been a mistake. She knew he wanted a relationship with her, he had tried before and feeling sorry for him was no basis for anything other than professional friendship. In the past, she had been more successful at holding the people she worked with at arm's length, but as the team became more used to each other the barriers had broken down. She enjoyed the friendship with Kate Lewis and valued the closeness she had with Charlie Lambert, which was still strong even though he was miles away on Merseyside.

Well, she'd committed herself and knew it'd be on her mind. She didn't have time or space for this stuff. She turned back. She'd get it over with before it became a thing. "Tomorrow," she said. "For a coffee."

"Oh, great, yes. The place we went to before?" He referred to a small café which served breakfast.

"Well, okay then. I'll see you there around sevenish."

She could meet him early, talk about the case then they would have to leave for their offices. There would be an automatic time limit.

She waved a hand at him and walked the short distance next door.

* * *

The neighbour was in her tidy living room, a glass of water and a cup of tea on the low table in front of her chair. The officer who had been left to support her was beside her on the sofa. As Tanya walked in, the PC stood and moved to stand near the door.

"Don't get up, Ms Cartwright," Tanya said.

"Elaine, please call me Elaine. It's Mrs Cartwright, my husband's away right now. Back next week." There was the quiver of nerves in her voice and as the woman spoke, she picked and plucked at the fabric of her black trousers.

"So, you're on your own?"

"Yes. I don't mind usually. Dave's away a lot and it's fine. I've got the dog, Mixie. She's in the garden now. I should take her for a walk." The woman realised she was gabbling and pressed her lips together.

"Is she a big dog?" Tanya asked.

"Not really, she's a cockapoo. But she's noisy sometimes."

"And last night?"

"No, she didn't bark or anything. If she had done, I would have looked outside. I would have seen Carol. I might have been able to help her. I let her sleep in my room sometimes. Mixie, not Carol." She laughed, a little embarrassed. "Maybe that was why she didn't cause a fuss."

The tears started. Tanya glanced at the police officer and raised her eyebrows. In response, she sat back on the sofa and leaned to pat the weeping woman on the back of her hand.

"I'm sorry. It's all been such a shock," Elaine said.

"Yes, I know. Please don't apologise. I think it would help you to know there was probably nothing you could have done for your neighbour. But now, the best way to help is to tell me everything you know about her. How well did you know her?"

Elaine shook her head, just once. "Not terribly well. Now and then we would have coffee together. She was on her own. Her husband died about six years ago. I didn't know him much at all. You don't, do you? When the men are out at work and with Dave being away, we didn't mix as a couple, not often. A glass of sherry at Christmas, that sort of thing."

"When was the last time you saw Mrs Barker?"

"Saturday, in the morning. She was hanging out the washing and we had a bit of a chat. I was cleaning up after the dog."

"Was there anyone else there – at the house?"

"No, I don't think so. They usually came later, afternoon, or in the evening during the week."

"Who were they, the people who came? Were they friends, family?"

"Oh no. She has a daughter, in Australia – I've given the other officer the details. Someone will have to tell her, won't they? How awful. What a rotten job."

"Yes, don't worry – we'll take care of it. So, who were the visitors?"

"Well, I suppose they weren't really visitors. Students."

"How do you mean?" Tanya asked.

"She did home tuition. Maths and science. For the SATs at the beginning but I think now it's GCSEs. The kids are older, they don't come with their parents. We thought it was good because it was annoying having the cars parked outside. Oh, listen to me, poor Carol is dead and I'm moaning about car parking. I'm sorry."

Tanya shook her head. "It's alright, don't worry. So, she was a teacher. Do you know which school?"

"Saint Matthews, she was there for a long time but once she lost her husband, she gave it up and just worked at home. She said she felt left out with all the younger staff at the school, they were all just starting out and she was coming to the end. They didn't include her so much, socially, you know. It might have been true, or it might have just been what she thought. She lost a lot of her confidence once he died, they had been devoted to each other. I don't think she ever really got over it. She was nervy, insecure really. She had to have tablets from the doctor and then she just gave up going to the school. Kids these days, they're not the same, are they? Oh, the little ones aren't so bad but these older one, with their backpacks and their hoods up. We used to wear uniforms.

She said it was very difficult keeping discipline and without anyone at home to share it with – well, I think it got on top of her."

The conversation was wandering now, and Tanya was beginning to think the neighbour didn't have much to offer. "Do you know how she found students? Did she advertise?"

"Oh, I don't know. Maybe, or maybe they were just from people she knew. As I say, we weren't close. I feel so bad now, I should have been a better neighbour. Seeing her there, under the tree in the rain…" The tears came again.

Tanya gathered her things together. "I'll have someone come by and take a statement, officially, but in the meantime, if you think of anything else, anything out of the ordinary, just let me know." She pulled a card from her pocket and laid it on the table, nodded to the constable and left the room.

* * *

Walking back into her office was like coming home. The other desk, the one that had been Charlie's and then later Brian Finch's was, yet again, empty, and dusty. But her desk and her chair with the wobbly caster and the view from her window out into the car park were old friends. She gave herself a moment to listen to the sounds of the building, already buzzing with life. She stroked a hand over the desktop leaving a line in the grime. No cleaners had been in during her suspension, but it was okay. She took a couple of tissues from her bag and rubbed away the film of neglect. She knew Kate would organise a landline for her, not that she would use it much, and a PC, though her laptop would be her favoured machine. She opened the drawer in her desk and took out her pen holder and her notepad, and then she left and walked down the corridor to speak to the boss. She was back.

As she reached the secretary's desk outside DCI Scunthorpe's office her mobile rang. She held up a finger as she clicked the answer button.

"Detective Inspector Miller, it's Moira. Doctor Hewitt will be performing the post-mortem examination at three-thirty this afternoon. Don't be late and allow time to change your clothes."

Before she could respond, the line was dead. So, Moira hadn't changed in the last couple of months.

* * *

The meeting went as well as she could have hoped. Bob Scunthorpe had always been supportive, but he expected his officers to work together and Tanya knew he was frustrated by her inability to always comply.

"I understand you've already picked up a case?" he said.

"Yes, sir. Only just back from the scene. DC Lewis is getting things sorted. Not much to tell you yet." She gave him what she had and then asked about Sue Rollinson.

"I understand she's sticking around for a while so she can just carry on. As for you, Tanya. Please try not to get yourself into a situation this time. Don't go off on your own. Don't get injured and don't let's be having this conversation again – okay?"

He tempered the words with a smile, but she was in no doubt that she was, in his eyes at least, still needing to prove that the recent investigation had come to the correct conclusions. It was added pressure she didn't need, but her own fault after all.

* * *

"Great to see you back, boss." Dan Price stood from his seat to come and shake her hand.

"Thanks, Dan. I have to say it's great to be back, though it might have been nicer to have a day or two without something like this." Tanya pointed at the whiteboard which had images of their victim and pictures of the house and garden.

They all paused as the door opened and Sue Rollinson-Bakshi walked in. "Hello." She raised a hand in greeting which took in the whole of the room, walked over to the desk she had used before and dragged the chair out as if there had been no talk of leaving.

Tanya judged it best to leave it for now. Later though, she would need to have a word with the young woman. They needed to agree terms and if she wasn't willing to toe the line and give the present case her full attention, then, despite the shortage of troops on the ground, she would have to go.

Chapter 3

"DC Rollinson, you're with me for the post-mortem. The rest of you join the house-to-house."

If the team were surprised at the speed with which Tanya slipped into her old role, they kept it to themselves. They just pulled out their notebooks and started making notes. She gave them the little information she had. "Kate, can you concentrate on trying to find out what there is to know about these students? How she found them, how many there were and so on."

As the team filed along the corridor, she raised a finger at Sue Rollinson and pointed towards the still empty office.

"Right, Suhita, we need a word. First of all, I'm pleased you've decided to stay around for a while…" She waited but there was no response, the other woman glanced around the room and then gave a little shrug. It wasn't going well.

"You and I have had words in the past about your approach to the work and the other members of the team."

Still nothing.

"Okay, cards on the table. I will support you, the same as I support any other colleagues and especially as a woman. However…"

Now Sue cocked her head to one side, but she still didn't speak.

"You need to focus. There's no room for…" Tanya paused, she had to be careful, it was easy to fall foul of all sorts of rules to do with discrimination. Sometimes it was hard to keep up. Damn it, she would just say what she had to. "Look, you need to leave the frivolousness for your time off. It's great for us to have drinks together, we all have to get on but – sometimes it sort of leaks over into your conduct at work. You tend, at times, to lose your direction."

Sue opened her mouth to speak, Tanya raised a hand. "I don't want to go into specifics, I think you already know what I mean. Charlie Lambert, and then Brian Finch."

"We never had a relationship."

"I know, but you really need to be more careful. Everyone noticed. If he hadn't already had a partner, it might have been understandable, but it wasn't on and apart from anything else, he is a higher rank and that takes it into really dodgy territory. I don't want you spoiling your career chances for the sake of a bit of a fling. It's not worth it, you're better than that."

The young woman pushed back the chair, her face red, her lips a tight line. "I take great offence at your accusations," she hissed. "I did nothing wrong." She leaned across the table. "I don't expect you to understand, you don't do friendly, do you? I was simply being a good colleague. I think maybe I've made a mistake deciding to stay. You say you're supportive but you're not, you work on your own. Every case I've worked on with you, you've gone off on your own, been more interested in scoring points for yourself than working with the team. I'm going to see DI Scunthorpe, now. This afternoon."

"And what are you going to say to him?"

"What?"

"When you see DI Scunthorpe, are you going to tell him you're offended and hurt and upset? Are you going to tell him you don't like what I've said to you? Think about it, Sue. Can you honestly say you have always been focused on the cases, the victims, your job, all the time? I think you know I'm right. Whatever you say to the DCI will be on your record."

They stared across the desk at each other and then slowly the younger woman lowered herself to her seat. "Before you came back, I made the decision to stay here, for a while anyway. I don't want to leave my family just now. But I think you're being unfair. You've made assumptions and yes, I'm offended."

"So, come on, really – what are you going to do? Are you going to throw your toys out of the pram and have a tantrum or maybe just think about what I've said?"

Sue Rollinson looked down at her hands twisted together in her lap. She took a breath. "For now, I'll stay. I'll work with the team on this case but as soon as possible I'm putting in for a transfer to another team. I'll show you."

"Good. Do that. Prove me wrong, nothing would please me more." Tanya stood and picked up her bag. "We need to go now; we can't keep Dr Hewitt waiting." As she spoke Tanya felt a twitch of nerves when she remembered the arrangement she had made to meet Simon in the morning.

Chapter 4

It was still raining. The ground was muddy and sodden. Jayden dragged himself up with his hands on the top of the tall, wooden fence between the house and the spare ground behind it. Not too far, he didn't know how many people were in the garden and he didn't want to be seen. The front road was still blocked by police cars and there were people in thin, all-in-one suits everywhere. Carl shifted underneath him, and he felt the fence wobble with the movement.

"Keep still, bro."

"You're effing heavy, mate, and you're getting mud on my jacket. What can you see? Hurry up."

"There's a tent thing under the tree, you know, where she was. There are still people everywhere. Shit, man, no way we're getting in there, not for ages."

"Oh crap. We have to. We really have to," Carl said.

When Jayden lowered himself to the wet grass his mate turned away, he brushed at the leather jacket and banged at the legs of his jeans. He dragged up the hood on his sweatshirt and Jayden knew he was really hiding his fears behind the action. He understood, perfectly. He was scared shitless himself.

They leaned against the damp wooden fence. "What are we going to do, Carl? We're in deep trouble. Gregor isn't going to want to hear that we couldn't get in."

"Aw, come on, he has to know how it would be. He'll see it on the news and he'll know. Look, I reckon it's all too late anyway. The place is crawling with cops. There's no way we are getting in the house any time soon and even if we did, there'll be nothing there now. Nothing."

Jayden tipped back his head and closed his eyes. "This is some bad shit, man. We can't go back, not empty handed."

"What else can we do? If we can't get in the house," Carl said.

Jayden pulled out his mobile phone. "I've had an idea. Let's take pictures – of the police and that. The cars and the tape. Then we can show Gregor. If he sees what it's like he'll understand."

"Nah, he won't. He won't be interested. He'll want to know why we ran away. It doesn't matter what we do – he'll be blaming us."

"I don't think I'm going back. I'm heading out. You should come with me."

"Heading out, where?" Carl said.

"I don't know. London, probably."

"But mate. What about your mum?" Carl was panicked, he felt the tears prickling again.

"I'll ring her. Once I'm away," Jay said. "Come. Just come with me."

"But Gregor knows where I live. Do you think he'll just give up? What about our Kayleigh? What do you think'll happen to her?"

Jayden shrugged and shook his head. "She's got to grow up sometime, doesn't she? Anyway, I'll bet she's not so much of a kid as you think. Not your Kayleigh."

Rain trickled through Carl's dark hair and dripped onto the front of his jacket, he sniffed and rubbed a hand across his face. "Okay, look, we'll get some pictures. This is all her fault, stupid bloody woman."

It wasn't, he knew it wasn't, but the blame had to land somewhere, and she couldn't fight back. Not now.

They walked across the spare ground, round the first corner and along the side road which took them to where the first of the police cars was pulled across the junction. The rain was heavier, coming down in sheets, blowing in the cold wind. Uniformed officers were drenched, their heads lowered against the deluge. The two boys stopped at the corner, one behind the other, hunched close together, they crouched behind the wall. Carl had his phone out, low down, videoing the scene back and forth – the vans and cars, the tape, the figures as they rustled in and out of the house in the baggy outfits.

It would have been okay if Dan Price hadn't arrived right then, through the gloom, splashing through the puddles sending a gush of water flying from the wheels of his car. The boys leapt back away from the spray. Carl's phone, slippery in his wet hands, skittered across the flagstones. He ran to where it landed on the kerb edge, saving it from the gutter.

"Oh, bugger it."

Dan slid to a halt in front of the flapping crime scene tape and opened the car door.

"Hey, sorry, lads. Sorry."

He began to clamber from the car, one leg out, his head leaning from the interior. "Are you okay?"

He pushed back the car door, twisted in his seat.

The youngsters glanced at each other, then at Dan. Carl grabbed his phone and they turned and ran, splashing through the lying water, feet slipping and sliding. Dan paused a moment, half in and half out of the vehicle. "What the hell." He glanced back in at Kate who had swivelled round to peer through the rear window.

"Little sods, probably getting some pictures to sell to the media. Let 'em go, Dan. Just let 'em go."

"Do you reckon?" Dan said.

"Yeah, come on, we've got enough to do."

"You're probably right. I feel bad though. I didn't see them. I must have soaked them through."

"I don't reckon they'll be making a complaint. Come on, let's get on."

With a final glance at the fleeing figures, Dan reached into the back of the car for the clipboard. "Yeah, okay. I'll start at number fifteen on this side. You take the ones over there. Start with the one that's being done up I reckon, catch the workmen before they finish for the day." He pointed across the narrow road. "Uniforms have done up to number thirty."

"Bloody rain." Kate took the sheet of paper he handed her and pushed it into her pocket. "See you later. With a bit of luck, there'll be old ladies with tea and cake."

"Yeah right, knowing my luck it'll be cleaners who don't want to let me in. I'll get the coffees afterwards, eh?"

"Make it hot chocolate and you're on. I hate post-mortems but I reckon Sue got the best deal, being with the boss."

Dan cast one final look down the road where he could just make out the two small figures, still running through the puddles. He hoped they'd have somewhere to go to have hot chocolate.

Chapter 5

"Exsanguination, I'm afraid. She bled out under the tree," Simon Hewitt told them.

He had cut and dissected and removed parts of the body. Weighed the organs and noted the state of them. He had dictated into his machine and finally left his assistant to make the victim presentable for whoever was to formally identify her. Tanya and Sue watched from beside the dissecting table. Not much to say until it was all over.

They sat in his small office afterwards, coffee delivered by Moira with a huff and a couple of tuts.

"If she had been able to get help, the medics may have been able to save her. Abdominal wounds are nasty, complicated, and painful, but sometimes they are survivable. Not in this case though," he said.

He shook his head sadly and glanced down at the pictures on the desktop. "What a terrible, lonely way to end your life. Who will identify her?"

"Well," Tanya said, "the daughter is in Australia and apparently there are no other living relatives in this country. I'll ask the neighbour. She's seen the worst of it. No need to traumatise someone else if she's okay to do it."

"I'll make sure she's ready. Just let me know when. I'll have my report to you as soon as possible. Tomorrow if I can. But, for now, what I can say is the knife was reasonably broad-bladed and heavy, about twelve inches long, partly serrated on the back which is a bit unusual. Used with some force. She tried to protect herself, there are defence wounds on the hands and arms. She had eaten before she died. Pork meat, some potatoes, and peas. There was a small amount of alcohol, probably just a glass of wine with her dinner. She had at least tried to hang on to some sort of routine. So many older people, once they are alone, manage with sandwiches and bits of cake, packets of crisps and now and then not even that, just cups of tea and milk, but our lady had eaten a decent dinner."

"The crime scene officers found crockery and cutlery on the dining room floor. There was a little food in the fridge and cupboards. Yes, she was looking after herself to an extent."

As she spoke Tanya clicked on her phone and held it out for Simon to see. "Looks as though she had just finished eating when she was attacked. Only one place setting, though, so she hadn't had a visitor for dinner. We are looking into the students she had arranged. When we find if any were due on Saturday it'll be a help."

"Well good luck, Inspector. She's fortunate you're here to work for her."

He opened his mouth again. For a moment Tanya thought he was going to refer to their arrangement to meet in the morning. She glanced quickly at the other woman who had reached across for a biscuit and Simon nodded and smiled.

"It won't be much help for her now but perhaps it'll help her daughter in the future," Tanya said.

"I'd like to know what you find out eventually if you don't mind." He stood and held out his hand. As they left his office, he was already dictating into his machine. Another name, another body.

* * *

"We'll go over to the scene. I'd like a walk around the house myself. The original examination should be pretty much done by now. You can join the others in the house-to-house if they haven't finished. I'll take the next-door neighbour. She may have remembered something now she's over the shock a bit. Anyway, I'll arrange for her to come here," Tanya said.

The DC grunted, made a show of pulling on her jacket, resettling her bag across her shoulder, and then stomped out into the puddly car park at the front of the mortuary. Tanya sighed and followed. She plipped the car key, slid into the driving seat and drove in tense silence towards Summerfield. She wasn't putting up with this for long, the other woman was going to have to sort her attitude or she'd be gone. It would leave them very short on the ground but would still be better than the atmosphere in the little car.

"There is no mention of a weapon being found, is there?" she said.

Sue scrolled through the report on her tablet. "No, the usual knives in the kitchen. A block on the worktop with all the slots filled. They have done a fingertip search in the garden but nothing there. It's spare ground over the back fence so they are going over it now. They've done bins and bunkers and what have you."

"Yes, Dave Chance'll have it all under control. If the thing is there to be found, he'll find it. Sounds nasty – heavy and partly serrated. I'm wondering about one of those zombie knives. It'd probably be worth researching them. I'll mention that to Dr Hewitt when I see him." She paused, wondering if she would get away with the slip.

"I can message him if you like. Ask him," Sue replied.

"Let's wait. Could be that Dave and the team will be lucky. If not, we'll make the suggestion."

There was no response and Sue clicked off her computer and turned to glare out of the window.

Chapter 6

They had used the trains without paying before. It wasn't difficult. Jayden watched until the guard was occupied with a woman with a pram and then they stepped on, heads lowered, shoulders hunched. The knack was not to attract attention but if young men in hoodies often were noticed, young black men were noticed especially. People moved a half step away, looked in the other direction, gripped their bags just a bit tighter. Nothing new, nothing to bother them.

They walked through two carriages until they found one less crowded, the passengers were busy, stowing cases, removing coats, and plugging in their electronics. The boys slipped through the sliding door into the little toilet cubicle and slid the lock.

Carl lowered to the floor and pulled out a spliff.

"Nah, I don't think you should do that. They'll have smoke alarms, won't they?" Jayden said.

"They don't work. Not with one little joint. Just waft the smoke about a bit. They never go off. Look, it's there. Just keep away from it," Carl told him.

They felt the train move, a couple of people tried the lavatory door and they hid their faces behind their hands to stifle the giggles. After a while, someone knocked.

"Hello – are you okay in there?"

There was a conversation on the other side of the sliding door. "I reckon it's out of order, mate. Nobody been in or out since Oxford."

It was agreed among the group outside that there should have been a bloody notice on it and the two boys settled back. They listened for the shout as the guard walked through checking tickets. They gave him a few minutes and then slouched out into the carriage. Ignoring the glares and grumbles of the other passengers, they moved on. The next toilet was occupied but the chances of tickets being checked again were low and they sat together staring out of the window. The train stopped at Leamington and they left. Trains were frequent and while they waited for the next one, they bought chocolate and Cokes. They climbed aboard, waited until it was on the way and then again hid in the toilets.

It wasn't far now; the chances were nobody would bother them. Unless some busybody complained to the guard, which was unlikely. This was England after all, people didn't make a fuss. Anyway, if it happened, they'd deal with it. They could say they hadn't had time to get a ticket. They couldn't talk except in whispers and there was little comfort sitting on the floor of the toilet cubicle but they had saved some money and, what was even better, they'd got one over on the train company.

When they reached Birmingham New Street, the last hurdle was the ticket collectors, but they'd done it before. They split up. Jayden lost himself in a large group of European students and pushed through in the middle of the crush. Carl, still high from getting away with the free travel and hyper from the tension of the past couple of days, vaulted the barrier and ran through the station. A transport cop gave chase for a short while, but the evening crowd was heavy, it was cold and wet, and Carl was younger, quicker, and more determined.

They met up under the bridge outside the station. They weren't ready to go home. There was stuff they had to sort out. McDonald's in Stephenson Place was open twenty-four hours. They bought burgers and chips, Coke to drink and sat at a table near the window. The restaurant felt grubby at the end of its busy day. The windows ran with condensation and the air stank of grease and stale bodies. Carl glanced around and wanted to go home. Home wasn't much but his room would be warm, and he could have a shower and change his clothes. He couldn't say anything to Jayden, but he missed the days when his mam and dad had been together. The house had been better, the food had been nicer, and his mam had washed his clothes and cooked stuff. She didn't bother now. Now his dad had gone, she worked hard, long hours in the big cut-price clothes shop and then she wanted some fun, out with her mates, drinking wine and coming back to the house late. Home to lose herself snorting the stuff Gregor supplied. The stuff that had led to tonight for Carl. Scared and sickened and trying to be tough in front of Jay.

At least his sister was probably safe. Kayleigh would be at her friend's house. She might as well go and live there. Okay – he knew why. Tracey's mum was a receptionist at the doctors'. A posh job with a uniform. And Tracey's dad worked in an office. Something to do with insurance. Their house was clean, there were cakes and they had a little dog.

Sometimes it was fun, out with Jayden, larking about, lifting stuff from Poundland – now and then something better from the department stores. But there was the other side. The stuff with Gregor, the stuff with the gang and now this. This thing he was trying not to think about. The woman under the tree, groaning as the rain fell on her and the blood leaked out; so much blood, slippery and stinking. He was tired. Tired and scared. Jayden was his best mate, but he didn't know what would happen when Gregor found out about everything. He couldn't be certain Jayden, even Jayden, wouldn't drop him in it and let him take the blame. This wasn't small stuff, people had disappeared, had their legs broken, had fingers cut off, ended up in hospital screaming and crying. The things they knew and the things they heard terrified him and he felt so lonely. Even here in McDonald's with his best mate. He didn't know what to do and he wished he was somewhere else. He wished he was *someone* else. He felt tears gather and he couldn't cry so he threw some chips across the table and laughed at Jayden as he pulled them from his hair, and they got up and charged out into the street running across the roads, dodging through the traffic and trying not to think about what they would do now. Too deep in to get themselves out. Too tied in to ever get free.

Chapter 7

It was late by the time the house-to-house was finished. Bad timing saw them going back and forth along the road as cars turned into driveways and lights were turned on in hallways and living rooms. In the end, they had spoken to most of the neighbours. Though they had left contact numbers, none of the team thought anyone had much to tell them. Surely if they had been aware of disturbance late at night, at the weekend, they would have mentioned it already. This wasn't a sink estate with frightened people refusing to answer the door to the police. This was a neighbourhood of coffee mornings and twitching curtains, Christmas drinks and litter picking.

Tanya sat with the next-door neighbour and Elaine Cartwright agreed to identify the dead woman the next morning. "I'll arrange a car for you. It's a formality of course and we'd be very grateful," Tanya told her. "Afterwards, if you need it there are support officers who can help you. With the trauma." She thought this woman, lonely without her husband, would probably use the counselling service. "Do you think maybe you should ask your husband to come back? Just for a few days until you are over the shock. Surely his company will understand. They sell stationery, don't they?"

"Yes, and greeting cards. It's so much harder these days, with all the online shops. It's hard and he's busy. He has sales meetings already arranged. I'll be okay, I'll contact your support people. I don't know how I'm going to sleep tonight though."

The woman's eyes filled with tears and Tanya asked the uniformed officer to make tea, but she left as soon as it was drunk. She'd done all she could. Tanya had the feeling that the drama was filling some sort of gap in the woman's life. Although she was shocked and saddened, the attention made up for some of the horror. For Tanya, though, who hated fuss, the proper work was waiting.

Back at the office, the team were cold and tired.

"DC Lewis will collate the house-to-house questionnaires, so make sure you get them to her in a readable and timely fashion. Kate, can you make sure you get everything from the uniformed officers who helped us out? Back in tomorrow for a briefing at half past eight. If anything has popped up, we'll deal with it then. We still don't have a weapon. We don't have an obvious motive as yet. I think one of the main areas of attention must be these students. It is imperative we get a list of the most recent ones as quickly as possible. I'll speak to Dave Chance and have his people keep an eye out for any sort of timetable, a diary, that sort of thing. In the meantime, we might as well call it a day. If anyone fancies a drink it's my shout. Might as well celebrate" – Tanya drew quotes in the air – "'being back'."

They all came. Dan Price only stayed for one drink but when he told her he was glad to be working with her again she could tell that he meant it. He also told her that he was about ready to put in for his sergeant's exam and he'd appreciate some time with her to discuss it. It made her smile. It also made her feel ancient. Sue Rollinson had a glass of wine and sat at the end of the table, quiet and sullen. As soon as Dan left, she also stood to go. Paul Harris dragged her back to sit beside him. He'd called his wife and she was on the way to join them. He wanted to make a night of it and if the party broke up too quickly, he'd be left with just the two of them. Not for the first time, Tanya wondered just how strong their relatively new marriage was. Cops marrying cops sometimes worked but cops marrying those outside of the job were bloody lucky if they didn't end up living apart, sharing kids at the weekends and niggling about whose fault it had been that it had gone wrong.

They drank enough to make it necessary to share taxis to get home. They ate barbecue ribs and chips in the pub, and when she let herself into her own house, Tanya was tired, a bit drunk, grubby, and the greasy food sat like a rock in her stomach. She wanted to curl into a ball under her duvet but instead, she did fifteen minutes on the exercise bike, took a long hot shower and only then did she crawl into bed. She propped her pillows behind her, booted up the laptop and went through all the images and as many of the written reports as had been sent through. Dave Chance had emailed to request a meeting first thing. Now then this was interesting. She fell asleep with the murder of Carol Barker playing in the front of her mind, right where she wanted it.

* * *

Breakfast with Simon was pleasant. He was already waiting when she arrived at the little café. They went through the preliminaries, then he filled the silence before it became too long and turned awkward.

"How are things with your sister?" he asked.

"Yeah, not too bad. I spent Christmas with them. It was better than I thought it would be. Serena is doing okay now."

"The resilience of youth. It's a wonderful thing."

"Well, that and the fact the bloke who abducted her is locked up."

"I'm sure it helps."

He asked her about her enforced leave. They chatted of incidentals as he ate his full English and she had a couple of croissants hoping they'd settle her stomach which was complaining about the excesses of the night before.

"You don't have any news on this new case, I suppose?" Simon asked.

"I had a message earlier from Dave, the scene of crime manager. He wants me to meet him at the scene in about…" she glanced at her watch "…half an hour. I know they've found a couple of diaries with some names and addresses. We are hoping something will turn up if we speak to the students. DC Lewis is going to the bank today to get access to the accounts. We are arranging a video call with Mrs Barker's daughter. Just in case her mother had been worried about anything. I have to say it's great now when we can speak directly rather than wait for written reports from local forces but, being Australia, timing is an issue."

"Well, good luck with it all." Simon glanced down at his hands, folded on the recently cleared table. "I've enjoyed this morning. It's been nice to catch up."

Tanya felt a flip in her stomach. *Please don't ask me for a date, please don't.*

She glanced at her watch again. "I guess we'd better get off. Can't keep the troops waiting." She began to gather up her things.

"Thanks for coming this morning. It's a great start to the day."

Now she felt guilty. Was he really so lonely that a quick breakfast in a steamy café was so special?

"I've enjoyed it," she said. As she spoke it surprised her to realise it wasn't altogether just a polite response.

* * *

Dave Chance was waiting for her, shifting his weight from foot to foot as she suited up. He led the way into the house, up the stairs and then ushered her forward as he came to a halt in front of a narrow door in the corner of the landing. There was a pile of clean towels on the carpet and beside them a couple of sheets, a pillow and two clean nightdresses.

"Nothing has been confirmed yet, shouldn't be long though. We've sent off samples."

As he spoke, he leaned into the airing cupboard. Tanya stretched forward to watch as he pulled out the bottom shelf.

"Do you see?" he pointed into the dark interior and stepped aside to let her nearer.

"It's nothing," Tanya said.

"Well, yes. It's a space. It's empty but…" Now he held up a small evidence bag. "This was caught on a nail."

"What is it?"

"A little piece of parcel tape and some polythene." He grinned at her, smug and satisfied.

Tanya shook her head. "Help me out here, Dave. I'm not with you."

He took the evidence bag from her hand and walked into the front bedroom where he held it up in the light from the window. "Now do you see?"

"It's grubby."

"Aha – but why is it grubby?"

She liked Dave but now he was irritating her, partly because of the mild hangover and partly because she knew he wouldn't waste her time so there was something of importance here and she couldn't see it.

"Okay, I can see you're not getting it," he said. "It's residue. As I say we are still waiting for confirmation, but I would bet my best pigeon it's drugs."

"Your best pigeon?" Tanya screwed up her face.

"Yes, Black Jack. I race pigeons. Don't say you didn't know?"

"I bloody didn't but… No, wait. Stop." She closed her eyes. "Okay, let's leave the pigeons for later. You're saying you think you have found evidence of drugs in the airing cupboard, in that space."

"Yup."

She walked back across the landing and peered into the dim interior of the cupboard. "Nah. Come on. She was an old woman, a schoolteacher. Shit, she was a widow. She wasn't a drug addict. It's just not on."

Dave shrugged. "I've found the evidence. Well, not me but one of my team, which is the same thing. It's up to you now."

Chapter 8

They had the notebooks, actual hard copies in evidence bags, and there were electronic copies of every page on the big screen which had been placed beside the whiteboards. The older books were filled with names, ages, and subjects. There were contact details and records about timekeeping and no-shows. They were obviously the lessons which had been booked. The children were young, all under the age of eleven.

"That's for their SATs," Dan Price said. "Before they go to senior school. We've also got these."

He held up a couple of bags holding A4 notebooks. "They are about the lessons, the progress – or not." He grinned as he placed them back on the table. "Some of the kids needed more than a bit of tuition by the look of it. But she kept good notes and any who did well in the exams have a jotting beside them and it seems that she wrote them a letter of congratulation. Seems as though she was a caring teacher, committed to doing a good job."

"There's nothing much since last June, is there?" Sue Rollinson said.

Tanya thought she seemed more engaged that morning. Maybe the get-together of the night before had helped to bring her back into the team.

"I suppose that's after the exams. Then it would start again with the next group, but it didn't." Dan swiped the screen. There were a few social events, a couple of doctor's appointments.

"Looks as though it all slows down. I thought she was supposed to be teaching older kids these days. The more independent ones that didn't need to be brought by their parents. According to the neighbour anyway," Tanya said.

"Perhaps she has a different system for them. Have we checked her phone and computer? I know they've been brought in."

"Good thinking, Kate. Can you get on to that? Chase the IT team and mention it to them. Maybe she moved onto an electronic calendar or spreadsheet," Tanya said.

"But this year's diary still has her doctor's things in, a couple of hospital visits. Just the dates and times. Birthdays for her daughter and the family in Australia." Dan was still scrolling through pages.

"Yes. What are we thinking? Maybe she wasn't doing the teaching anymore?" Tanya said.

"It's possible, isn't it, that as she lost contact with the school, it became more difficult to find work. We still haven't found any adverts. Nothing in the local library, the shops or anywhere. Nothing in the church hall. We highlighted it with the house-to-house team and the crime scene officers, and they came up blank. I'll task one of the civilians with calling the local newspapers, the free magazines and the like and speaking to the advertising departments. I can't think of anything else unless it's online. I'll see what I can find." Kate was making notes on her laptop as she spoke.

"Perhaps they were past students. You know, just keeping in touch," Dan said. "I still talk to some of my old teachers when I go to my sister's school plays and things. I go to the assembly if any of them retire."

Tanya wondered what it would be like to be so comfortable with your family history that you still visited your old school; still held on to the past. She had kicked it into touch as quickly as she could. Once she signed up as a cadet with the force, she left home, at first to live in the section house. Later, out of the blue, a bequest in her grandfather's will left her the money for a deposit on her own little house, where she still stayed.

She nodded at Dan. "It could be, I suppose. Or maybe it's the neighbour confused. I'll have another word. She's identifying the body today. DC Rollinson, will you come with me and we'll see if she's up for another chat. Now then."

She clicked an image of the small evidence bag onto the screen.

"This is a new thing. I don't know what it means yet. I need your thoughts. It's out of left field and, though I have some ideas, I would appreciate input." She told them the little they knew and was met with blank stares and puzzled frowns.

"I'll leave that with you. Dan, can you go through the diaries in greater detail. Paul, the bank is expecting us, I think Kate has enough to do, would you take that? Then we need to go through all her accounts. Okay, I'm heading down to update DCI Scunthorpe and then I'll meet you at the mortuary, DC Rollinson. Kate, can you organise some of the civilians to start calling the parents of the students whose names we have. Ask them to try to get a feel for how the kids liked her. Whether the mums and dads were satisfied with the tuition. Surely if she did a good job, they would have passed her name on to other families. Let's see if there was any dissatisfaction, you know, students who didn't do as well as they should have done."

Tanya paused. "I suppose we should address the elephant in the room. If there is any suggestion at all of any sort of abuse, sexual, physical, mental, then we have to get on to the specialist team. I really hope there isn't anything like that but if we don't address it, we could come unstuck further down the line. Be discreet but keep it in mind. It seems unlikely that an older woman would be involved in something like that, but we all know it happens and we really can't miss that if there is anything."

Chapter 9

Carl tried calling Jayden over and over. They were going to meet up and go together to see Gregor. All night he had been awake in the bedroom. He had tried watching stuff on his computer, played Fortnite, smoked some of his stash. He was scared and panicked, and he wanted it over. Gregor was going to blame them, it was obvious. He wouldn't want to listen to their excuses and explanations. Then again, he might not even talk to them.

It was becoming light. He could hear Kayleigh moving about in the bathroom and then running down the stairs. He'd go and get some breakfast with his sister and then try Jayden again. It was unlike him to have his phone turned off. Carl tried to eat some of the cereal. He looked at his sister. She was pretty, he saw that. He teased her but there was no doubt about her looks and her figure. The lads eyed her up as she passed them and a couple of them had made comments – he'd sorted them. She wore her clothes to draw attention to herself, her skirt waistband rolled to make the thing shorter. He knew she sewed her school blouses so they hugged her figure tighter, showing off her boobs. He looked away. It embarrassed him to be looking at her and thinking this stuff. She was his little sister and the comments Jayden had made about what Gregor might do made him feel sick and the corn flakes stuck in his throat. He gulped down some milk and had to run for the lavatory to be sick.

He heard his mum in her room. He had been home before her the night before, even though he and Jay had stayed in town until the pubs closed and the drunks rolled down the streets. They had walked back. It was a good long walk but there was no rush. When she came in, he heard her in the kitchen, his mum, talking to herself and then in the living room knocking things over, swearing. He hadn't gone in. He'd done it before and scraped her up from the couch and helped her into bed. That night, though, there had been the image of the other woman, the one under the tree, bleeding and groaning, and it was all his mum's fault. If she had left the blow alone, if she'd stuck to booze and fags then Gregor wouldn't have been in their lives and Mrs Barker would still be alive. Daft old bat.

He couldn't face school, but he had to put his uniform on and set off down the road with Kayleigh. If he didn't, his mum would be on his case. Nagging and whining and ignoring the fact that, really, all the problems stemmed from her.

He felt bad when he had these thoughts. Times like this he believed he hated his mum and it was wrong. It was always wrong. His dad had to take some of the blame, him and the slapper he'd gone off with, had another kid with. That had broken his mum more than the shop work, the shortage of money, the bills. The other baby. Women were odd and he didn't understand them.

They arrived at the school gates and Kayleigh went off with her giggling, hair-flicking mates. She didn't even look back to see where he had gone. He walked away, just one glance back. A few of the lads he used to be mates with were there, going in through the metal gates, uniforms on, backpacks full of books. He didn't bother to carry his anymore. There was no point.

Mr Kimble, the headmaster, drove past. He glanced through the window and Carl saw him shake his head. He gave him the finger and turned, walked a bit quicker to get to the stop just in time and jumped on the bus to town.

He sat upstairs at the front. Spread himself, laying across a double seat, so he didn't have to share, and he tried Jayden again. There was still no answer. They were supposed to meet with Gregor down near the market. He'd head off there. Jay could be there already.

It was busy in Birmingham. The shops were open, and the centre was full of workers and people heading to the big new station and the shopping malls. The rag market wasn't open, but the outdoor market was. He bought a sausage roll from a stall and went to sit on the steps by the church. A couple of cops on bikes passed. They clocked him so he got up and waved to a woman coming across the precinct by the war memorial. He pretended to walk towards her, and they rode away. By the time they had pedalled up towards the Bull Ring, he'd marched past her and she never knew she'd been used. It was nearly ten o'clock and time to meet – either Gregor or whoever. There was still no sign of Jayden. Carl was really panicked now and when his phone rang, he felt weak with relief.

The number was withheld but Jay did that sometimes. He wasn't sure why and he was so glad to get the call that he didn't give it much thought. Not until he heard Mrs Gormon. "Carl, is that you?"

"Yes, Mrs Gormon. Is Jay sick?" There was a moment of silence.

"Is he not with you, Carl?"

"No. I was waiting to meet him."

"Are you not in school?"

"No. It's a free period, study time, you know." The lies were easy.

"Okay. When did you see him?"

"Last night. We were together last night. We'd been in town." It wasn't a lie, not really. "We walked home together."

"He didn't come home, Carl. I thought he'd stayed at yours. I don't know where he is, and he isn't answering his phone. If you see him will you tell him to ring me straight away? I need to speak to him."

"I will. Yes, I will."

He clicked off his phone and tried the number for Jayden. He'd done it, hadn't he? He'd gone to London and what was worse, he'd gone on his own.

He spun three hundred and sixty degrees, peering into the growing crowd. There was no sign of Jayden, but he could see, at the end of the street, Gregor's black SUV pulling into the kerb and the blokes clambering out of the back.

Chapter 10

The Skype call to Australia was arranged for just after nine and by then Tanya had read the overnight reports, had a quick catch-up briefing with the team and spoken with the civilians who were helping with the house-to-house enquiry reports.

There was nothing new. Nobody had seen or heard anything. They all knew the older lady who lived alone, some of them remembered her husband. They said hello to her now and then.

The house, three buildings away, where the contractors were working was unoccupied. Being done up before it was sold. The owner had died over a year previously. The note by the uniformed officer was brief. Baylies Property were the contractors. George Roberts and Stewart Dawes were the guys on site. They normally left at five and started work at half past eight. They had witnessed the arrival of the police and ambulance and really hoped it wasn't going to interfere with the work. Scaffolders were arriving on Wednesday with a big vehicle. They had seen nothing – knew nothing. They had been antsy and difficult.

"Nice of them to be so concerned," Tanya said.

Kate simply shrugged and continued to read the notes.

* * *

Mrs Barker's daughter was pale and red-eyed. She was pretty if you ignored the ravages of grief.

"Why would anyone hurt a lovely lady like my mum?" Stella Barker said.

Tanya nodded. "That was going to be my first question. You don't know of anyone who your mum had perhaps had a row with, nothing like that?"

"No, she kept herself to herself. Since we lost my dad, she'd sort of shrunk into herself. I felt guilty, being so far away but…" The woman shrugged.

"When did you last see her?"

"It's over three years since I really saw her, but I had a video call with her last week, on Thursday. We had one every week. Not always on the same day and sometimes, it was just to say hello. But it was every week. I can't believe I'll never talk to her again."

Tanya waited until the young woman regained control. "How did she seem when you spoke to her? Did she seem worried or upset at all?"

"Not really." There was a short pause. "Although, to be honest, I've been worried about her for a while."

"Oh, how come?"

"She's seemed a bit… distracted somehow. I was terrified it was dementia. Sometimes she wasn't herself and she had trouble concentrating on what I was saying. I had sort of suggested she go and see the doctor. It's difficult though, isn't it? You don't want to offend people."

Tanya didn't have a response. In all honesty, she didn't know. She had never dealt much with old people and not offending someone wasn't really an issue with her. If something needed saying she said it. It had caused trouble between her and her sister, between her and her colleagues, but she didn't know another way to do things and truly didn't see anything wrong with being open and up front.

"Did she? Did she go and see the doctor?"

"If she did, she didn't tell me."

"We will go and have a word. If she consulted her doctor, she might have said if there was anything worrying her."

"She hasn't always been like that. When she was working, she was a brilliant teacher. Confident and happy. The kids all loved her, and she was great with them. There were some difficult times at her school, but she was great at handling it all. It was after dad died, she started to fall apart. She gave up work. I told her I thought it was a mistake and to give it time. She wouldn't listen though."

"What do you know about the students she saw at home?"

"She enjoyed it for a while. But she gave up earlier in the year. After the last lot had done their SATs."

"So, you don't know about her tutoring older children?"

"No. She always did juniors."

"Do you know why older children would be visiting her then? Young teens?"

Stella Barker shook her head. "No, she never said anything. Nothing about teaching older ones. She was planning on coming out here anyway, so I don't see why she would start something new. Maybe she was feeling better. She used to like teaching the older kids, back when life was… well, when it was normal. Mum said they were more challenging and that was rewarding, watching them sort themselves out she called it. She was coming for a few months. I'm pregnant."

The woman glanced down and moved her hand towards her belly.

"She was going to come for when the baby was born and stay for a bit to help, but a couple of weeks ago she said she wasn't sure she could come. She wouldn't say why. Just that maybe it would cost too much. I offered her the money for her fare, and she wouldn't hear of it. She'll never even meet her grandson now, will she?"

The last comment was effectively the end of the conversation. The woman couldn't recover enough to carry on. A tall man appeared on the screen, crouching down behind the chair so he could be seen.

"I'm Ollie. I'm Stella's partner. I think she's had enough now. If you want to talk to her again let us know. But not today, not just now."

"Thank you, erm… Ollie. Thanks. We'll find whoever was responsible. We will find out and get justice for Mrs Barker."

She clicked off the screen and sat for a moment, the image of the weeping woman playing in her mind. This murder had spread its filthy tendrils quite literally to the other side of the world.

She walked to the whiteboard, made a couple of notes, and then turned to Sue Rollinson. "Come with me, will you? The crime scene first and on the way find out who Mrs Barker's doctor was and get us an appointment. The neighbour I spoke to again yesterday at the mortuary insisted that there were young people turning up."

Then, turning to the others, she said, "The rest of you find a motive for this. Someone knew this woman and the kids that were visiting. I want to know why."

Chapter 11

"You never said you were sorry," Sue Rollinson muttered.

"What?"

"When you spoke to the dead woman's daughter. Most people would have said they were sorry. You just got straight into it. Don't you think it would have been nicer?"

"What difference would it have made?" Tanya said.

"Well – it's just what people do, isn't it?"

"Is it? Well, as I say it wouldn't have made any difference. She's lost in her own grief right now. I needed information from her and coming on all sentimental wouldn't help."

"It's just the kind thing to do, that's all."

"Yeah, well, being kind isn't going to find this murderer, is it? I would appreciate if you kept your opinions about my manners to yourself, DC Rollinson."

The atmosphere was horrible, thick with resentment and Tanya was tempted to turn around and take Rollinson back if that wouldn't have seemed totally juvenile. She huffed out a sigh and turned on the local radio to listen to the request for information that the press office had arranged.

She didn't want Sue trailing behind her when she did a walk-through of the house. She didn't want her there at all and the feeling it was going to be better to cut her losses and have the woman transferred was becoming more pressing despite the brief hope of earlier. But she was there now, so she had to use her.

"I want you to go back and have another talk to the contractors. They are here all day unlike most of the neighbours. They might have seen something they didn't realise was important. Perhaps an unfamiliar car, someone hanging around. Go and have another word. Perhaps they'll take a plain-clothes officer more seriously than they did the uniform."

"Yes, ma'am."

The response was low and sulky. She knew she was being pushed aside. The idea had been to inspect the crime scene, not to talk to grumpy and difficult workmen.

Once the car pulled into the kerb, Sue Rollinson clambered out and stomped away towards the refurbishment project which was rapidly disappearing under a web of scaffolding. They were unloading the metal poles, the wooden walkways, and other equipment. She probably should keep away, and Tanya knew that she should call her back. But as she watched the slender figure storming off down the road, she shrugged her shoulders and went to the taped-off house on her own. There was no officer on duty at the door because the crime scene team had finished their work. She knew anything of immediate interest would have been taken away, but it was the first chance she'd had to walk uninterrupted around the place where the dead woman had lived and to get a feel for the sort of life she'd had.

The key she held was for the kitchen door at the side of the house. A cardboard label hung from the keyring. Everywhere inside was smeared and dirty with fingerprint powder. There were streaks of blood on the walls and across the tiles.

Already, after just a couple of days, the home felt abandoned and forlorn. The sofa cushions had been removed and piled on the floor and in the master bedroom the bare mattress was askew on the divan frame.

It was obvious the house had been relatively well maintained, though the paintwork on the doors and window frames was dried and flaking here and there. There were scuff marks on some of the walls. How much was due to the investigating team it was difficult to say. In the kitchen the cupboards were stocked with some tins of soup, vegetables, and packets of dried foods, but the shelves were sticky and grimy. The cooker needed cleaning. There was a feeling of moderate neglect which spoke to Tanya of someone who had given up trying. In the wardrobe the clothes were out of fashion and there was a vague odour of staleness as though some of the things needed to be washed. They would speak to Mrs Barker's doctor and Tanya was sure they would be told she was being treated for depression. She must have Kate check what the contents of the bathroom cabinet had been. She'd seen this before when she worked in the missing persons unit. So often it had ended with the sad discovery of someone who had decided they had nothing left to give them joy and had committed suicide. But this woman hadn't killed herself and any chance of recovery from her ennui had been stolen from her.

The visit had been useful even though there was nothing startling to be found. Indeed, there shouldn't be if Dave Chance's team had done their job, and she had never known them not to. Tanya felt she understood the woman a bit more. She glanced at the door to the airing cupboard. She must chase the lab results for the strange find in there. She peered into the small space. Nobody had replaced the bottom shelf and she put a hand into the gap but there was nothing there now but dust and grit. She turned and started back down the stairs.

The noise from outside was loud, but when she heard it Tanya wasn't particularly alarmed. The cries that followed were of more concern and she hurried through the house, locked the kitchen door, and jogged along the side path.

A couple of people passed her, running along the road.

The scaffold company truck was drawn partly onto the pavement, illegally, but no-one was going to take it up with the burly men she had seen earlier. As she ran closer, she saw the small crowd, workmen and the people who had run past the house. They were ashen-faced, staring at the pile of debris in the front of the house. There was a heap of wooden walkways, plastic barriers, and sundry building junk.

In the growing confusion, Tanya began to search, her eyes flicking back and forth, looking for her detective constable. She dragged out her phone and scrolled down until she found Sue Rollinson's name.

Chapter 12

Carl hadn't waited around. As Gregor's men climbed out of the car, he cast one last desperate glance back and forth, but Jayden was nowhere. He turned and ran back across the precinct, up the stairs beside the church, and out into the main drag. He turned right at the top, down Queensway past the shops, and on to the multi-storey car park. He turned right and right again, glancing back to reassure himself the thugs weren't after him.

He jumped the ticket barrier at Moor Street station and slid between the doors of the train standing at the platform. He didn't sit down, he stomped through the carriages back and forth until they pulled in at Small Heath. Once out of the station he jogged through the houses to Small Heath Park. He was starting to feel safe, which was stupid in a place like this. As far as he could see there was no-one around and he sat on the floor in the bandstand, his back against one of the pillars. He couldn't stay here, not at night, not on his own, unarmed. He didn't belong and he didn't need anyone else after him. It seemed he had escaped Gregor's thugs for the time being, but he couldn't stay and couldn't go home now.

He dragged out his mobile phone and tried Jayden's number again. He had a glorious moment of relief when the call was answered. "Jay, man, where are you? Your mam's looking for you. Gregor was down in town. I ran away." He was about to blurt out his location and some sixth sense shut his mouth. He listened. He knew there was someone on the other end but all he could hear was the slow in and out of someone breathing.

He cut the call and stared at the phone in his hand. The silence had been more frightening than watching the thugs clambering out of Gregor's big car. It wasn't something he could run away from.

He tried to swallow but his mouth was dry. Thoughts crowded in, terrible thoughts, he pushed them away. His hands shook and cold, sticky sweat plastered his body, he shivered. He glanced around. A small gang of lads walked down the path from the children's play area. They were older than he was – taller, stronger. He didn't wait for them to swagger any nearer. He pushed to his feet and ran for the exit onto Tennyson Road.

He was in a mess, he didn't know what was happening with Jayden, he couldn't go home in case Gregor or his mates were waiting for him. He couldn't go to Jayden's house for the same reason.

He could go to his nan's but then if he was found there, he was dragging her into the whole shitstorm, and he couldn't. At the thought of his nan, the only one who had really had any time for him, the one who had come to his school plays and bought him a new blazer when all his mum could manage was a manky thing from the charity shop, he felt the sting of moisture in his eyes. No, not his nan.

He pushed back into the shadows under the trees as a car passed. It was a big car, a Beemer, four blokes inside, music thumping loud. He couldn't stay here, not when every car caused his guts to clench and bile to rise in his throat.

None of this was his fault. Not really. It wasn't even Jayden's fault, but he'd never be able to explain to Gregor. All he would be interested in was what they owed him, what they had of his.

He couldn't get his breath, he had a pain in his chest; shit, he really couldn't breathe. His fingers were tingling, he felt dizzy and sick. He was going to die of a heart attack here on the grubby floor outside the park. If Gregor found him now nothing would save them, none of them, not him or his mam or Kayleigh. He was nothing, nothing more than a transport system, taking stuff back and forth, a delivery donkey, stupid and as good as dead. He curled down into a ball under the tree and let the tears come. Gasping and choking he sat on the damp floor and wished, more than anything he had ever wished for before, that he was at his nan's house, watching one of her stupid soaps and eating toast. Where had it all gone? How had that turned into this? His mam, that was how. His mam and her habit and her debt to Gregor that they had decided he would repay. He was swept with anger so strong that it overtook the panic attack and brought him back to his feet.

He would go. Jayden had been right. It was the only thing to do. He turned and walked back along the road. For a long time, all he did was wander the streets, his thoughts batted back and forth: London, sleeping rough and all the dangers that represented; not going, and everything that would mean. He bought a couple of chocolate bars and a bottle of water and sat in the doorway of a deserted shop, his back pressed against the peeling wooden door.

As dusk fell, he went back, through the houses, past the lighted windows with their stop motion glimpses of families together, watching telly, eating their tea, and he went back to the station. He'd get the next train to Birmingham. He pulled his wallet from his jeans pocket. There was money in there. He had some money, they always had some now, he didn't like to think where it came from, but it was good to just have it. He'd go to Grand Central and decide once he was there where he was going to go.

Chapter 13

They wouldn't let Tanya in the ambulance. "Sorry, ma'am, we need to be able to do our work. Follow us in your car. We'll take your friend to the Radcliffe."

"But is she okay? Will she be okay?" The small body of Sue Rollinson being pulled from under the debris had horrified her.

"I'm sorry, love." The paramedic leaned and put his hand on her shoulder. "You need to let us go. Come to the Radcliffe. We'll look after her."

Tanya turned away and called Kate. She gave her a sharp, fast account of what had happened. There was silence at the other end then she heard Kate clear her throat before she was able to respond. "She's okay, though?"

"I don't know. I don't think she was conscious. By the time they got the debris away from her the ambulance was here, I couldn't get close."

"How did this happen?"

"I don't know, I really don't. I was in the house. I had sent her to speak to the workmen." She took a deep breath, squared her shoulders. "I need someone to go and tell her family. I don't want them just getting a phone call. Do you know them, Kate?"

"No, I don't. I don't think any of the team really know her family. Charlie has met them. Back in the day when she was new to his team."

"Well, he can't go, not from Liverpool. Do you think you could do it, Kate?"

"I will, boss. I'll take Dan with me."

"Yes, yes that's good. He's good with people."

"Let us know what you hear though, boss. It'll take us about half an hour to get to her home. Listen, it'll be okay. I'm sure it'll be okay."

"I don't know, Kate. It didn't look good. They put her on a back-board, there were drips and a collar and what have you."

"Yes, but they always do that sort of thing. Come on, she'll be fine."

Tanya couldn't answer. Kate hadn't seen the way the paramedic had looked at her. She hadn't seen the small form on the gurney and the expressions on the faces of the workmen who had dragged the board away and thrown it aside in the grass. They were still there, standing in small groups, smoking, and shaking their heads. She had to get it together. First thing had to be to find out what happened. A patrol car arrived with the ambulance, but the officers had been busy keeping bystanders out of harm's way and clearing a route for the emergency vehicle.

Tanya walked over to them. She pulled out her warrant card. "I want you to secure the site. Get the names of anyone working here. Don't let anyone leave."

They frowned at her. "Yes, ma'am."

"Some of my team will arrive soon. We will need to interview everyone."

She had pulled out her phone. So, Kate and Dan were on the way to Sue's home. There was only Paul Harris. It wouldn't be enough. She called him. Cut off his question and told him they'd need help. "Speak to DCI Scunthorpe.

Tell him the situation and ask him for some help. I have to find out what has happened, while it's still fresh in the minds of the site workers and before their own investigation team get here confusing things, covering their backs and what have you."

"So, you're going to the hospital?" Paul asked. She could tell by the sound of his feet and the change in his breathing he was already on the move.

"Quick as you can, Sergeant." She cut the call.

The ambulance disappeared in the distance.

She believed Sue was unconscious. Following to the hospital would result in her drinking horrible coffee for hours in a corridor somewhere, waiting, just waiting.

She closed her eyes.

She walked towards the nearest group.

"I need to know what happened. Did any of you see?"

The man she recognised as the lorry driver turned. "Who are you?" He glanced at the wallet in her hand. "Oh, right. Shouldn't you have gone with your friend? George says she was a cop, the girl."

"Yes, she is. I brought her. She works with me. I need to understand what happened."

"We're not sure yet. I didn't really see. I was round the back, having a coffee. The erection team were busy up the other side."

"So wasn't anyone here? Doesn't anyone know how it collapsed?"

"Well, it didn't, not really. If you look, the staging is sound here. It's the boards that fell. The boards and some equipment on it. She was just bloody unlucky to be where she was."

"But how could that happen. Isn't it fixed?"

"Yes, of course it is when it's done. But they were in the middle of it. She shouldn't have been here; nobody should have been standing there. I don't know what the hell she thought she was up to. Sorry and that, I realise it's your colleague, but I just don't see what she could have been doing there."

"She was looking for Stew."

"Sorry, you are?"

"George. We talked to your oppos the other day, me and Stew. About that thing down there." He pointed in the direction of Mrs Barker's house.

"I told her, that girl that got hurt, I told her I hadn't seen anything, and she had to talk to Stew. I said she should get out of the way, that it was dangerous. I gave him a shout. Next thing I know there's a yell and a shutter and the whole bloody lot is there on top of her. Shouldn't you go and see how she is? We'll have an inquiry, sure to, and we'll find out what happened. But isn't she your mate? Shouldn't you be at the hospital?"

"Where is he? This Stewart."

"He's there." They glanced towards a small white van. "Oh, he was there a minute ago. Well, I suppose he's pretty cut up. He'll be about somewhere." The bloke sniffed and shook his head. "Don't mind me saying but I hope if it was my mate, they'd be more bothered about me than some poor bloody contractor who's probably in shock." With a cough and a hawk, George threw his cigarette to the floor, stamped on the end of it, grinding it beneath his boot, and then turned and stomped away.

Chapter 14

By the time Carl arrived at Grand Central the rush hour was over. The place was quieter. Most of the trains now were local ones and they were no use to him at all.

His first instinct was always to try and get on without a ticket, they often did that, and he enjoyed the buzz, but tonight he didn't want any more stress. He'd buy a ticket. To buy a ticket he'd need to decide where to go. Okay, the final destination wasn't important, he could nip off anywhere.

He watched the departure board. Cardiff – that was Wales, wasn't it? He didn't want to go there, it was all hills and sheep. Hereford, he hadn't a clue where that was. He needed somewhere big, a city where there would be cafés and stuff. He wasn't sleeping rough. That wasn't him. Him and Jay had tormented the rough sleepers, thrown chips at them, harassed them. No, he wasn't one of them. He probably had enough for a room somewhere, a cheap bed and breakfast. It was just until he found Jayden and they had a plan.

The departure board changed. There was a train to Oxford. He wondered about the house. He wondered about the key which was always hidden in the shed. The police wouldn't be there now, would they? It was ages since they had found the woman. Okay they would search the place, it stood to reason, then they'd leave it. It'd have police tape all around it. That was good, wasn't it? With that around it he'd be safe, nobody would come in. He could stay there free. Nobody would know. It was only for a night, possibly two, after all. She kept it nice and clean and he'd have a proper bed. There might even be some food if the filth hadn't nicked it all. Plus, if he was thinking like this, surely there was the chance that Jayden had already had the same thoughts. He could be there, right now he could be waiting, with some cider and some hash. The more he thought about it the more he was convinced. Either Jayden was there now, or he would come there as soon as he could. Bloody hell, they might even be able to find out what had happened. Of course. He lifted his head, squared his shoulders. Back at the house, that's where he'd find his mate.

He bought a ticket. He stopped at a stall for a couple of slices of pizza and a can of drink to take on with him. He was pleased with this idea. If, when he got there, the police were still hanging around he'd go and find somewhere else.

He rang his mum. He told her he was staying with Jay. She sounded spacey already. "Is Kayleigh home?"

"No, Kayleigh's not home, is she? She's never bloody home. She's with that friend of hers. Some homework or something."

"Is she coming home tonight?"

"Well, I don't know do I? She never bloody tells me anything."

He felt the anger start to rise and clicked off his phone.

"Kayleigh, it's me. It's Carl. Are you at Tracey's?"

"What's it got to do with you?"

"Aw, come on – don't be a dork. Look, I'm not coming home tonight. I'm with Jay." It was a small lie and would preclude any questions. "I just rang Mum and she's already pretty messy. Can you stay with Tracey?"

"I might."

"No, listen, Kayleigh, tell me you will. Stay there and don't go home, don't walk on your own. If you can't stay there get an Uber. You can put it on Mum's card. I'll give you the number."

"What are you, my jailer?"

"Listen, Kayleigh. Jay and me have got into a bit of a fix. Just stay there or at least be really careful and don't walk home, and don't go on the bus, yeah?"

She picked up on the urgency in his voice, he heard her sigh and then murmur. "I was going to stay anyway. We're colouring our hair. But, Carl, is Mum okay?" She sounded young now, young and a bit scared.

"Yeah, just messy, you know. She'll be fine. Look, I'll see you soon, but it might be a couple of days. Okay?"

"Yeah, okay."

"Oh, and, Kayleigh, don't tell anyone I rang."

"Are you okay, Carl? I mean, you're not in trouble or anything?"

"No, 'course not. We just have some stuff we have to do. Important stuff."

"Okay. I'll see you in a bit then."

"Yeah. See ya, Kay."

He pushed the phone into his pocket and fought back the stupid feeling of loneliness and worry. It was all going to be okay. All he had to do was find somewhere to doss for the next few days, get in touch with Jay and then they could work out what to tell Gregor. They had to tell him something. It wouldn't be safe at home until they had a story for him. It had to be good, and they must work out what it would mean, for him, for Kayleigh and for his mum.

He boarded the train and pushed into a seat in the corner, his brain was spinning. He was tired and confused and scared. He leaned his head into the corner and closed his eyes. They were filled by the picture of the old woman lying on the grass under the tree, her hand pressing down on her stomach while the blood seeped out.

Chapter 15

The atmosphere in the incident room was gloomy. The civilians muttered together quietly and turned away when Tanya glanced at them, suddenly finding stuff to do on their screens. She let them go home.

"Back in tomorrow and we need to make some progress." In truth everything had ground to a halt. The parents with children who had studied with Carol Barker had reported they were happy with what she had done. A couple of them were disappointed with their kid's exam results but even they didn't blame the teacher. Results had come in from the lab confirming Dave Chance's suspicions about the residue on the scrap of plastic. *'Black Jack is safe'* he had written. Another day it would have made Tanya smile but not today. She noted the information in her book and on the whiteboard. It was puzzling. Possibly the daughter had taken stuff, it was something she needed to ask, and she made an entry in her diary to book another Skype to Australia. That could be a tricky conversation, but at the moment she could think of no other explanation. She assumed Simon Hewitt would have ordered a tox screen but maybe not given the age and cause of death. She made another note to double check with him. They had to cover all the bases no matter how obscure.

The team had pulled their chairs together. Dan Price looked red-eyed and anxious. Paul Harris made a couple of abortive attempts to lighten the mood but gave up when it went nowhere. Kate tidied Sue's desk, throwing away the takeaway mugs which had been left since the morning. She wiped the surface with a tissue and lined up the papers. She wiggled the mouse on its mat and leaned in to look at the screensaver. She didn't know Sue's password and leaving the force logo floating on the blue background felt wrong. She uttered an expletive and clicked it off again. She picked up the landline, listened for a moment to the dial tone and then replaced it.

"They said they'd ring my mobile." Tanya wagged her phone back and forth.

"Oh, right. Yes, of course. Her mum was in bits," Kate said. "I felt so sorry for her."

"Maybe we should have stayed longer," Dan said. They had sat in the waiting room for hours until Sue's brothers had arrived to support their mother and they felt superfluous and left.

"I thought you would have come, you know, to the hospital. Or even gone with the ambulance," Kate said, nodding towards Tanya.

There it was – the first hint of blame.

"I will. I'll go as soon as we hear she's out of surgery. As soon as there's a chance, she'll know I'm there and can answer questions."

"Right," Kate murmured.

"I needed to talk to the builders. It was important to find out just what had happened. Apart from that, we've still got to make some progress with this case. It was the whole point of us being there, wasn't it? It's what she was doing."

"Well, what did you find out?" Paul Harris swivelled his chair to face her directly.

"According to the blokes I spoke to, nobody knows how come the stuff fell from the scaffold. She shouldn't have been standing where she was."

"It seems bloody odd though, doesn't it? Great planks of wood don't just take it unto themselves to fall from a great height. There was no wind."

"I know. There will be an investigation though. The Health and Safety Executive and our own Health and Safety team will work together. DI Scunthorpe will keep us informed. Look, there's nothing we can do about that now. We'll find out what happened. But I sent her. I asked her to question the builders about the older kids. They have been there a while and it could be helpful. I had a go at them, but they were all too shocked for me to get anywhere with that…"

"Bloody hell, boss. I would have thought you would have been as well." Dan shook his head, pushed to his feet, and stomped out of the room. Tanya looked round at the rest of them and saw the same accusatory look in their eyes.

"Well, of course I was upset. Naturally, I was. But at the end of the day, the best thing we can do for DC Rollinson is to keep on working on this. Her accident will mean so much less if it all comes to nothing. Do you not see?"

Kate leaned down and picked up her bag. "I'll be at home. Will you ring me if you hear anything?" She didn't wait for an answer as she left the room. As the door swung closed, Paul Harris pushed back his chair and, without a word, he followed her.

Tanya glanced around at the empty desks, the debris of the awful day and at Sue Rollinson's scarf hanging on the back of her chair. Tears gathered in her eyes and she swiped them away impatiently, poured a cup of stewed coffee from the machine in the corner and walked through to her own office.

She rang the hospital, but they would tell her next to nothing. In the end, the nurse on the other end of the line softened and told her that in effect there had been no change. "Your friend is still critically ill. She has been out of surgery for an hour or so and her family are with her."

"But will she be okay? I mean, when will she be able to speak to us? What is wrong with her, exactly?"

"I'm sorry, I'm limited to how much I can tell you. She has a number of internal injuries. Her spleen was ruptured for one thing – we have removed that. She also has a punctured lung. Apart from that she has a nasty head injury and that is our main worry. You really should talk to her family when they have had a chat with the doctors."

Tanya leaned on the desk and hid her face behind her hands for a while. It was no good, she might as well go home, there was nothing further to accomplish here.

Back in the house she put on some soft clothes, opened a bottle of lager, and lay on the sofa. She drew in a deep breath and then reached for the landline.

"Charlie. It's Tanya. Listen, mate, I have some bad news for you. It's about Sue Rollinson-Bakshi."

Chapter 16

Charlie was upset. Although Sue Rollinson had caused him problems with her obvious attraction to him when they worked together, he had a soft spot for the young DC.

"There's nothing you can do," Tanya told him when he suggested he come down from Merseyside. "I'll let you know when she's out of danger and conscious."

They talked a while longer about the cases they were working on, and the politics of the force. Inevitably there were stories about Joshua and Carol and, although babies weren't her thing, Tanya smiled. She had met the little boy and Charlie's devotion to his son charmed everyone.

After hanging up the phone she sat in the quiet house. She should work, eat something, but she didn't have the energy. The disapproval of her team was upsetting, more than she would have thought. She sort of understood. But sitting beside an unconscious woman wasn't going to get them anywhere and they still had to work for their victim.

She poured a glass of whisky and carried it with her upstairs to her dressing room. There were a couple of new jackets she hadn't worn, and she wondered if, maybe when she was better, Sue would like one of them. Sue's large family had never had money to spare and she often admired Tanya's outfits. She pulled them out and folded the dark blue blazer into a bag. She would take it into work and show Kate, tell her it was a present for their injured colleague.

She looked down at the parcel at her feet and acknowledged the embarrassing truth. She was looking for what her mum had always called 'cupboard love'. Trying to buy her colleagues' approval. She shook her head and put the coat back on its hanger.

* * *

Next morning, the team were in early, most of the civilians were there and they were passing around a large 'Get Well' card. Everyone had written a short message, there were smiley faces and kisses and cute notes. When Dan Price brought it into the office Tanya wasn't sure what she should write and ended up simply signing her name.

"We're having a whip round for some flowers," he said.

"Oh yes, right. Of course." Tanya fished in her bag for her wallet and was mortified when there was nothing there but a couple of pound coins. "Sorry, Dan. I usually use my card. I don't carry much cash. I can go later to the ATM." As she said it, she knew her card was overdrawn, and the machine might well refuse her.

"It's okay, boss. I'll just take that shall I?" Dan reached out and took the money.

"Sorry, what has everyone else put in?"

"It's okay, don't worry about it."

And she knew they had all contributed more. Now she wished she'd brought the jacket.

The phone rang, she stared at it. This wasn't good news, she knew, she almost always knew. It was Bob Scunthorpe's secretary.

The woman had given nothing away but the sense that something was badly wrong had been palpable.

* * *

"Tanya, come in. Sit down."

She usually refused but this time, the look on his face, the lowered gaze unnerved her, and she perched on the edge of the seat in front of his desk. It was still very early days in the inquiry, surely, she wasn't going to be side-lined already.

Bob placed his hands on the desktop, the fingers linked. He sighed and then raised his gaze to look directly at Tanya. "I have bad news." He paused. "I have just taken a call from Mrs Rollinson-Bakshi. Her daughter died about an hour ago. She never regained consciousness. There was nothing they could do."

Tanya was literally speechless. She wanted to say something. Something appropriate, but no words would form. Bob waited for a moment and then nodded. "It's a shock, terrible. There'll be an inquiry, an inquest of course. Health and Safety, theirs, and ours. Have you written your report?"

Now there was a question to answer, she found her voice. "I have started it, sir. I don't know much. I wasn't there. I was in the house. Sue – DC Rollinson – was supposed to question the contractors. We hoped – well, I hoped, they would be more forthcoming to a detective rather than the bloke in uniform. Also, there was a chance they had remembered something. We were trying to find out more about these older boys. The teenagers."

"Alright. Make sure you have it all down. There will be other issues going forward but for the moment I'll leave it up to you to tell the team. Tanya… handle it carefully. They've worked together for a while now."

"Yes sir. I will. It'll be okay." She knew he doubted her abilities with personnel. She knew he had cause.

She walked down the corridor back to the incident room. The hum of voices leaked through into the corridor. With a deep breath she reached out and opened the door.

As it swung inwards, Brian Finch turned to look at her.

Chapter 17

Finch held out his hand and Tanya touched it briefly. "Detective Finch."

"Miller. It's good to see you. Shame it's under such circumstances. I heard about DC Rollinson-Bakshi. Thought I'd pop down to the hospital. They probably won't let me see her, but I can leave a message, she'd know I'd been. Just thought I'd come to see the troops first. I brought some breakfast if you're interested." He waved a hand towards the box of pastries on the table by the window. Dan Price stood beside it chewing at a chocolate croissant.

Tanya moved past him to stand in front of the boards. "I'm sorry. Everyone, could I just have your attention. I erm…" She heard a gasp and was aware in her peripheral vision that Kate had flopped down onto her chair. She knew.

"I've just come from a meeting with DCI Scunthorpe. He informed me that DC Rollinson, erm… Sue. Sue has died." She didn't know what else to say and as the hubbub broke around her, she turned to look at the images on the whiteboard. The notes and pictures swam and blurred as tears swelled. She swallowed hard. "Case meeting in an hour, I think. Give us all time to…" She rubbed a finger under her eyes and turned to walk from the room. As she passed him, Paul Harris lifted a hand towards her but dropped it back to his side as she swept through the door and down the corridor to her own office.

She booted her laptop, opened her book, and began to check the overnight reports. In the background was the quiet hum of voices, the occasional thud of a closing door and the sound of someone sobbing receding into the distance, as footsteps clicked down the corridor. She stopped pretending to read and pushed the chair away from her desk, swivelling it towards the window. Out in the car park, cars splashed through the puddles as the new shift moved into their day. A couple of seniors in fancy uniforms were dropped at the door and scuttled inside out of the drizzling rain. It was all very normal.

Sue was dead.

There had been other deaths to confront. Her parents, her grandparents and then the ones to do with her job. Children whom she had searched for when she worked in the missing persons section. That was always hard. The victims of her past murder cases, that had been hard too but the drive to do something, to get justice had been the stronger emotion. But this had been a bloody accident, a stupid senseless accident, with Sue in the wrong place at the wrong time.

She turned back to the desk and opened the report she had begun the day before. She read it through. There wasn't much to it. She had sent Sue to talk to the builders, she heard the noise of the falling scaffold.

Now she was dead.

She lay her fingers on the keyboard and waited for words to come.

There was a single knock on the office door. Kate had brought coffee. She moved into the room without a word and sat in the visitor's chair.

"Thanks." Tanya picked up the mug and wrapped her hands around it. "What's it like, in there?" She nodded in the direction of the corridor.

"Emotional. Some of the civilians were tearful. I sent them away. Told them to come back when they felt better. Dan and Paul are going through some of the house-to-house reports. They haven't said much. Finch is loitering round the boards. He tried to start a conversation about the case but, to be honest, right now I haven't got the time for him. I don't know what he's doing here. He wasn't very nice to Sue when he was with us. He knew she had a bit of a thing for him and he used it. Poor bloody girl, she was so naïve." Kate coughed, then covered the break in her voice by taking a sip of her own drink.

"It's my fault." Tanya had been fighting the thought and surprised herself as she verbalised the idea.

"Don't be daft. Of course it's not. It's just one of those things. One of those horrible things that happen."

"No, there was no need for her to be there. I only sent her down to the building site because I was irritated with her. She was supposed to be in the house with me. It was the reason we went to the scene. She knew as well. She knew I was just giving her something to do because I didn't want to be with her. We didn't need to question the builders again."

"Are you sure? I mean, that's not like you. You don't do things just for the sake of it. If you sent her to question them, you must have had a reason. You're not thinking straight right now. We're all upset."

Tanya shook her head. "No, I know what I did. I sent her down there because I was annoyed and irritated and if I hadn't, she wouldn't have been there. She's dead because I was impatient."

Kate stood and moved towards the desk and as she did the door swung open and Brian Finch was there, coffee in one hand, his briefcase clutched in the other. "No point in me going to the hospital now, is there?" Neither woman answered him.

He pulled up the chair from the second desk, the one that had been his. "You're going to be short of help, Tanya. I'm available, you know, if you like. Just put my last thing to bed, I could step in. I've been looking at the reports. I've got some ideas. You know, maybe with all this upset a fresh pair of eyes will help. I could make some calls. Have it cleared. We've worked together before. Okay, I know we didn't always see eye to eye and of course there is the rank difference between me and Rollinson but surely it's better than a stranger coming in. What do you reckon?"

Of all the things she might have wanted right then, Brian Finch was just about the worst she could imagine.

"I've already left a message for DCI Scunthorpe, he's sure to see the sense of it. Me being familiar with the area, the rest of the team. Anyway, look – I'll go and review what you've got and then, if you decide you can use me, well, just let me know."

Tanya waited until the door had closed before she spoke. "What's that about then?"

"May I speak freely, boss?" Kate asked.

"Of course."

"I believe he's having trouble settling in up in Birmingham. They took him there for his language skills and, as it turns out, they really don't need him. They have plenty of officers with second and even third languages. I think he might have bitten off more than he can chew, and he's rattled a few cages, from what I've heard."

"Right, well, I don't see how that means I have to have him back. I need to speak to Bob Scunthorpe before he has a chance. I know he's connected but we're not free parking, are we? Bloody hell, as if there wasn't enough to deal with. We still have to keep going, Mrs Barker still needs us to work for her. They do understand, don't they? I mean, we have to keep going."

"Yes, boss, of course. They need a bit of time, that's all."

"Yes, I expect you're right, but the best thing is for us to keep on working, isn't it?"

"Give them time, boss. Just give them time. We all have to deal with this in our own ways."

"Do you need to go home or anything, Kate?"

"No, I'm with you. Keeping busy right now is best. I have a couple of things that have come in overnight. If you want to deal with them now."

"What have you got?"

Kate pulled out her tablet. "I have a report on the residue found in the crime scene. Cocaine, apparently. Quite pure. The lab is working on finding out where it came from if they can. There is a very small amount, but they are giving it a go. There's nothing on the plastic or the tape, it's very common."

"Right, thanks. Can you get on to the morgue and ask Moira if a tox screen was done on the victim?"

"Yeah. What do you want to do about Sue's family?"

"How do you mean?"

"Well, you'll be going to have a word, won't you?"

"Oh, should I?"

Kate simply bent her head to one side and pursed her lips.

"Yes, of course I should. Can you arrange it for me? I'll go to the hospital or their home. Whatever's best for them. God, there's going to be a funeral and all of that as well, isn't there."

"Yes, boss. I think HR will have some input. If the family want something formal, with her uniform hat on the coffin and that sort of thing, they'll organise things. But I should think everyone will want to go anyway."

"Yes, of course. Erm, can you help me with it, Kate?"

"Of course, boss. Of course. I'll let you get on and make some calls to the family. I'll let you know what's arranged."

As Kate reached the door Tanya spoke. "Kate, thanks."

"No problem, boss."

Chapter 18

Carl was cold, tired, and hungry. He had been unable to reach Jayden and when he rang Kayleigh from the train, she had mocked him, dismissed him with a just a couple of curses. He heard her giggling with Tracey as she clicked off the phone. At least she was safe, and it was unlikely she would be going home now at after nine at night. He crossed the spare ground and pulled himself up on the fence. Mrs Barker's house was to the right of where he was, and it was in darkness. Of course, Jay wouldn't have the lights on if he was inside. He had more sense than that. He scuttled along the soggy grass and pulled aside the loose fence panel. Though the shed had obviously been searched, the police hadn't found the key which was slipped under the roof felt in a corner at the front. He pulled it out. He ignored the nagging thought that if Jayden had already come the key would have been missing. Possibly he was the first, or maybe Jay was out somewhere scoring some dope, getting a Maccy D's. Anyway, he was here now, and it had been the best idea. Jay would come, he had to.

Skirting the edges of the garden, he made a crouching run for the back door. Down behind the big wheelie bin he paused and listened. There were no lights inside, but the streetlamp cast a yellow flood over the side drive and the pavement beyond the gate. It was looking good, but he needed to be sure there were no coppers around. One had been stationed at the front door. Was he still there?

The tall fence which ran part of the way down the path became a short wooden railing nearer to the front. He pulled up his dark hood and pressed close along the edge. Slowly he crept forward. There was no policeman by the gate or the front door. The piece of tape still stretched across the front gatepost cracked and snapped in the breeze.

Now he crossed the narrow driveway to the house wall and leaned to peer down the street. He could see no-one around except by the house that was being done-up. It looked as though there was tape on the gatepost as well and a police car parked opposite. He couldn't make sense of it. Had there been another killing? Had he been wrong about what had happened? Could it be there was some madman prowling the neighbourhood; some lunatic bumping people off? The thought chilled him as he glanced behind into the dark wet garden.

If that was true, though, what did it mean for him? If it hadn't been to do with Gregor and Jayden and the couriering, it changed things. It changed things for the better. Perhaps. Events beyond his control. Maybe it was all to do with the woman. Just an ordinary robbery. How could he be blamed for that? Some nutter robbing and then offing innocent householders. Then again, nobody, no ordinary burglar would have found the stash of drugs or the money, it was well hidden, they had been careful about that, always. He'd never told anyone. Had Jay? Surely not; he was just as clued in about what would happen if they let Gregor down by blabbing their mouths. He needed to process this. He needed to talk to Jayden. He needed somewhere quiet and warm and dry.

The back door opened smoothly with his key. He turned on the phone torch and stepped inside. It was warmer than he had imagined it would be. Nobody had turned off the heating. It smelled odd. Not like when the old woman was there; then it was always cooking, or coffee or sometimes flowers. Now it was chemical, and he thought maybe blood. Yeah, and there was the stale, old person smell he had started to notice lately at his gran's house, a weird shut up thing because windows weren't opened, and corners weren't cleaned properly. He flashed his light around. There were dark stains and he knew what they must be. Stuff was out of place; the old woman had kept it tidy and it just didn't look like her house anymore. He stepped over the marks made by the blood and moved through into the hallway. Careful to angle the light downwards, so it didn't shine out through the glass in the front door, he reached the bottom of the stairs. Up on the small first landing he stopped to look out of the long window. Apart from the fuzz in their car down the street, at the end, there was nothing else. He opened the door to the bedroom at the front. Inside was a double bed and some old-fashioned furniture. He'd look tomorrow in daylight, there might be stuff there he could take. Would the police take her jewellery – if there was any? Maybe not and anyway there could be other stuff. Antiques maybe, though he wouldn't know what was good and what wasn't. Tomorrow he'd look. He wasn't sleeping in there; it was too weird.

One back bedroom was an office furnished with a couple of desks and chairs. Books on a bookcase, posters on the wall. The room next to it was cold but there was a single bed, a small wardrobe, a dressing table with mirrors. His torch illuminated the glass and showed him a dark figure, hooded and round-shouldered. He looked cowed. He turned away and threw his bag into the corner. He was hungry but most of all he was tired to the bone and shivering in this room. There was nothing on the bed, but in the top of the wardrobe he found a duvet; it smelled musty. Never mind. When he wrapped it around himself the warmth was lovely. The radiator began to heat when he turned the knob. Yes, this was okay. He thumped the dusty pillows and lay on his side.

He couldn't stay here tomorrow. He'd have to go into town or something. Just because the police weren't here now didn't mean they wouldn't come back. He didn't know how this sort of thing worked. Had they finished with the place? What would happen next? Now his brain had started thinking again, the other stuff all rushed in. Where was Jayden and most of all what was Gregor planning? There was too much. His mind began to race as sleep slipped away.

With a sigh he pushed into a sitting position and leaned his back against the headboard. He didn't want to disappear. His life had been pretty crap up to now, sad, and scary at times but it was all he had. He wanted it back. If he could get it back, then he'd straighten things out. He'd make his mum get help with her problem. He'd get away from Gregor, somehow. It would be hard, but he could do it. The other option, heading for London – not much money, no friends, nothing – he would end up as flotsam. Was that the right word? He thought so, it meant rubbish anyway and it's what he would be. Rubbish with no future and no life at all. Tomorrow he had to start to fix this. The shivering was easing, and his muscles softened. He dozed propped against the corner with his arms wrapped tight around him clinging on to the old quilt.

Chapter 19

The Rollinson-Bakshi house was a tidy, well-maintained semi. Sue's mother had taken onboard all the lessons learned in her job as an estate agent. The garden was gravelled and dotted with matching pots planted with boxwood balls. The front door was painted a tasteful burgundy and the drapes at the windows were tied back neatly. It was early and the leaves were still dripping from the overnight rain but through the windows they could see the lights were burning. The family had probably been up most of the night before. Experience told them that sleep was elusive in the face of shock and grief and often relatives welcomed any diversion from their swirling thoughts. Anyway, Tanya just wanted this done. Her stomach clenched at the thought of it. Kate had parked at the kerb and sat for a moment in silence after turning off the engine. She closed her eyes and shook her head. "This is probably going to be grim. Are you ready?"

Tanya leaned down to pick up her bag from the footwell. "No. But waiting won't help, so we'd best get on with it. But, thanks, Kate. I would have got to this in time, I reckon, but would have left it too long. You gave me the push, I'm grateful."

It wasn't as bad as it could have been. The family were dignified and calm. Sue's mother was gracious, but her face was ravaged and her eyes red-rimmed and sore-looking. Tanya and Kate said all the things expected of them.

"She was so impressed with you." They sat in the stylish living room. There were flowers everywhere already and sympathy cards on the side tables and bookshelves. They could hear Sue's brothers muttering quietly together in the kitchen. Sue's mother tipped her head to one side as she gazed at Tanya.

"From the first time she worked with you. She would tell us all about what you had done. Of course, she was careful and didn't say things that we shouldn't hear, but your bravery, your independence, they were how she wanted to be. It made her sad sometimes because…"

There was a pause.

"Well, she so wanted to be like you and yet, somehow she felt that she always fell short. She told us that you were supportive of women in the police, told us that you advised her about her way forward. I can't thank you enough. You made her want to take herself seriously and have some self-belief. She had a way to go. I know it was the case, and she knew it also." The slender shoulders shrugged. "Maybe if she had time, maybe she would have…"

"I'm sure she would. I really think she had the makings of a good detective. She was trying, wasn't she?" As she spoke, Tanya felt Kate turn to look at her, she saw her nod slightly.

"We all liked her. Her colleagues are heartbroken by what has happened," Kate said.

"Do you know yet, how it happened? Why it happened?"

"Not yet," Tanya said. "There will be a full inquiry and we will make sure you are kept informed. At the moment, it seems it was just a dreadful accident and I am so sorry."

"I have the contact number here for the human resources people, but they will be in touch with you very soon anyway," Kate said. "They'll help you with any arrangement but please, if we, Sue's colleagues, her friends, can help in any way just let us know."

"Just find out how this happened to my daughter. Maybe some good can come of it, lessons for people to learn."

"We will," Tanya said.

It was over and they were back in the car. "Shit, that was hard," Tanya said. "All the stuff about how she admired me and wanted to be like me. We didn't get on. I was irritated by her, I thought she was flighty and silly."

"Yes, well. Maybe keep that to yourself for now, boss."

"What? Oh, yes of course." Tanya blew out her cheeks. "I can't do this stuff. You do it so well, Kate."

"You did okay. They appreciated you going."

As the car pulled away from the kerb Tanya clicked on her tablet computer and began to scroll through the overnight reports. "Bob Scunthorpe wants to see me. Can you drop me at the front door? I'll go straight up."

"Yes. What time are we having the briefing? I need to make sure everyone's in and up to speed. Not that there's much to tell them. Things seem to be at a bit of a standstill right now. There're the drugs though. We need to follow that up more, don't we?"

"Give me thirty minutes. That should be enough I reckon and yes, see if there's any more information about the drugs. I wonder if it was the daughter's stash. From when she lived at home. A little hidey-hole that her mother didn't know about. We'll probably need another call to Australia but let's get more information before we do that."

"What are you going to do about DI Finch, boss? Is he on the team now?"

"Not if I can help it. Maybe that's what DCI Scunthorpe wants to talk to me about. I'm going to do everything I can to stop it."

* * *

Bob Scunthorpe's office smelled of coffee. The aroma had Tanya's mouth watering, but she refused a cup; she didn't want to stay. She didn't want to sit but he waited for her to take the seat he had offered.

"I'll not keep you long, Tanya. I know you're busy. I believe you've been to see Detective Rollinson's family?"

"Yes, sir."

"Good. I'll be going along later myself. You've got a lot on, and you were already short of staff. I think you need back up, just in case."

"In case?"

The DCI sighed. "I don't think it will come to it but if the investigation shows any sort of…" He paused. "Problem – with what happened at the building site."

"How do you mean, sir?"

"Okay, let me put it this way. DC Rollinson-Bakshi was working under your supervision. I am convinced in my own mind everything is as we believe, just an unfortunate accident. However, she was in the wrong place at the wrong time. If it's decided you must attend an inquiry, clarify things… Well, we can't have you taking your eye off the ball with the murder without adequate back up."

Tanya had been trying to ignore this niggle, the idea that she would be held in some way responsible. But then, hadn't she already said as much to Kate? *I sent her there.*

"As luck would have it, DI Finch is available." He held up his hand as Tanya began to stand, opened her mouth to protest. "I know you two don't see eye to eye, but you'll still be running the show. He's back-up, that's all, just in case. I'm sorry. I know you won't like this, but I judge it to be wisest at this juncture. He will need to share the office with you as before but I'm sure you're both mature enough to make it work. I hope this won't be for long and it's only until we have clarification on Sue's accident. I have to be sure we've covered every angle." He pulled a file folder towards him and nodded at her. "Thank you, Detective Inspector. Keep me apprised."

Chapter 20

The briefing was awkward and tense. Tanya wasn't sure how to handle things and defaulted to business as usual. Brian Finch didn't attend, and she avoided any reference to the investigation into Sue's accident. She had nothing to tell them anyway. Once she had updated them about the discovery of the drugs, the team were sent back to view CCTV again. The civilians were tasked with rechecking the house-to-house questionnaires to find what they might have missed. Anything that would give them a lead. It was dull and boring, and she could feel the buzz being lost. The first twenty-four hours was well past, they had made no progress and now they were all focused on Sue's death. She had to find a way to get them back on track.

She took Kate to one side. "Finch is joining us. There was no way around it. But what I reckon is that I can have him review Sue's accident. I'll tell him I want someone independent of all interested parties. That'll suit his ego. It'll keep him out of our hair. Right now, I'm going back to the house. I want you with me. Detectives Price and Harris can hold the fort here. Ten minutes in the car park."

"Why do you want DI Finch to look at the accident?" Kate asked, her face creased with puzzlement. "I thought it would be Health and Safety – ours and the builders. Surely that's enough."

"Just meet me in the car park." She turned and stomped into her office leaving Kate looking a little hurt. Tanya was unsettled, there was a worm of worry in her gut. Thoughts began to spiral. She pushed them aside. Her first duty was to Mrs Barker and she was getting nowhere. For the sake of the victim, and the distraught girl in Australia, she couldn't fail.

* * *

They had a key for the front door but before they went in Tanya wanted to go into the back garden, to see the tree again and trace the path that had been marked out. This was where a dying woman had dragged herself. Why? Was it to escape further attack? To try to get help? Something else entirely?

"She must have known she was badly hurt. It was raining and there is no way out of this garden except through the side gate. Why didn't she escape by the front door? At least that way there would have been a chance of finding someone to help," she said.

"Perhaps the door was locked." Kate referred to the report on her tables. "Hmm, it was unlocked when the first responders arrived. Maybe the killer was out there. Could be, she thought there was more danger out in the front than round the back. Or maybe it was just instinct. Maybe she was just trying to run away, and this was quickest."

"Why didn't the killer come out here though? Why not make sure they'd finished her off. Apparently, she bled for a while lying under the tree. What made the killer leave her?"

"Good thought, boss. Perhaps the killer was disturbed. Maybe a car outside or something. The neighbour said she hadn't looked out and none of the nearby houses report hearing or seeing anything but, well, maybe." Kate moved to the side passage and together they entered the house. The rooms were in disarray, things had been taken away to check for DNA, drawers lay on the floor with the contents disturbed, some of them piled on the carpet.

"God, it's depressing," Kate said. "I wonder what will happen. The daughter can't come from Australia, not pregnant. Maybe I could find the details of a cleaning company and help her to arrange to have it sorted a bit. In case she wants to sell it. Probably have to be redecorated."

"Not your job, Kate. We have people who can help with that."

"No, I know it's not but– well, surely our job is to help in any way we can, and we've already made contact."

"Our job is to find the killer. Housekeeping, cleaning – it's someone else's responsibility. Nothing to do with us."

Kate shook her head. "I'm sorry, boss, I don't agree."

There was a tense silence until Tanya shrugged her shoulders and headed for the hallway. "Do as you please then. As long as it doesn't interfere with your work but you're letting sentiment get in the way." As the words left her mouth, she regretted them. She knew she had a reputation for toughness, but that had sounded simply mean and heartless.

Kate was behind her, still in the living room. Tanya turned, intending to soften the impact of her words.

The noise from upstairs was soft, indistinct, nothing more than the shush of feet on carpet. Tanya froze and held up a hand in warning. They listened, there was the quiet click of a door lock. Tanya stepped up a couple of stairs. As she did all hell broke loose. With a screech like a banshee a dark figure threw itself downwards towards her. Half jumping, half falling, it collided with the two women who had begun to run upwards. One arm flailing, and a backpack whirling from the other hand, it was all noise and movement. Feet kicking, it barged past them, the dark hood was pulled up and forward. Kate screamed out as the bag slashed across her face catching her eye and spinning her away to fall back the couple of steps she had mounted. Tanya whirled round to follow and tumbled on top of the other detective, leaving them both in a heap in the hall as the front door was wrenched open and the boy, for they could see it was a boy, flew onto the narrow path, raced out into the roadway and away.

They staggered to their feet. "Are you okay?" Tanya gasped.

"Go, boss – I'm fine."

They chased but it was obvious very quickly they had lost him. Kate grabbed her Airwave unit to raise the alarm but all they could say was that it was a dark figure, probably male, slight in stature and with a backpack. The patrol car at the end of the road was facing the wrong way and by the time they had screeched to the junction to turn and speed back, the boy was long gone. Kate's face was bleeding from a cut at the side of her eye and a red wheal slashed across her cheek, her lip was already swollen to double the normal size and all they could do was stand in the road peering into the distance as the rain began again.

Chapter 21

He didn't know where he was going but Carl ran as far and as fast as he could. When the stitch in his side and his pounding heart got the better of him, he vaulted a low metal fence and ran into a copse of trees beside an ornamental lake. He flung himself to the ground panting and sobbing.

Proper sleep had eluded him for much of the night. The alarm on his phone had sounded but he had turned it off and intended to sit for just a few minutes and the next thing he heard was the sound of voices in the garden, the front door opening and then those two women jabbering on in the rooms downstairs.

Gradually, his breathing slowed, and he dragged out his mobile phone. The charge was low now, just over ten percent and he needed to find somewhere to charge it. He should have done it last night and the fact he hadn't made him angry, he cursed at the little device. He tried Jayden – still only voice mail. He hung up quickly. He called his sister and got no response. He called Tracey.

"Can you tell my stupid sister her phone's off, Trace?"

"No."

"Oh, come on, don't be such a cow – I need to talk to her."

"Well, she's not here, and don't call me a cow, you dork."

"Where is she then?"

"What, am I her mother? She went home last night. She was being a stroppy bitch and we had a row. She can sod off – I don't need that negativity."

"Shit. What time did she go? Did she get an Uber?"

"I don't know, do I? It was late, we'd done our hair and the stupid mare didn't like the colour. Listen, Carl, she's not my problem." She hung up.

Carl tried again to reach Kayleigh but there was no response. There was no other option and he rang his mother's landline. When the answering machine chimed in, he left a short, curt message. '*It's Carl. Kay, call me as soon as you can.*'

His phone was almost out of charge now. He turned it off. Until he found a place with a charging point, he could only risk turning it on to see if there were messages.

"Sod it." Bloody Kayleigh. He'd told her, hadn't he? He'd warned her not to go. Well, it wasn't his problem. She could look after herself. Anyway, what were the chances of her being in danger? It had been Jayden who had suggested it and sometimes he talked shit. She'd be fine. He needed to look after himself now. He needed to decide what to do next.

He clambered back over the fence and straightened his clothes. He glanced around. The road was empty except for a woman jogging off into the distance. This was a posh area, big houses, and expensive cars but he had to get to somewhere to charge his phone and have something to eat. He turned right simply because it was the opposite direction to the jogger and began to walk.

The stop wasn't far, and he hopped on the first bus that came. It was for the town centre and he sat in a seat near the front in order to nip off quickly if he needed to.

He was glared at by a young woman because it was supposed to be reserved for old codgers and cripples, but he didn't care and scowled at her, twisting his mouth into a sneer. She looked away to stare out of the window.

Cornmarket Street. He could see the golden arches. At least he knew what there was to eat there and he could use the toilets. He crossed his fingers and stomped down the road along with the early morning shoppers and the kids on their way to school.

Once he'd picked up his order and found a seat near the window, Carl took the charging cable from his bag and plugged it in. He turned on his phone. His heart jinked: there was a message from Jayden.

> *You need to come and see me. G*

The fear had been in the back of his mind from the start and now here was the proof he'd been dreading. *'G'.*

Gregor had Jayden's phone. Gregor had sent a message, not Jayden. So, where was Jayden?

The bite of burger turned to sand in his mouth. He grabbed the cup of Coke and tried to swill down the food. The liquid and the half-chewed bread and meat caught in his throat and there was no option but to spit it out. He aimed for the little box, but part of the gooey mess missed and splattered onto the tabletop in front of him. A child across the aisle made a squealing noise and pointed at him.

"Mummy, that boy spitted!"

The young woman glared across at him and screwed up her face in disgust. A cleaner with a dirty mop swiping at the sticky floor turned and stared. She glanced at the box and at him and over at the counter where the manager was peering over the cash register. This was spiralling out of control. Carl unplugged his phone and with a leer at the child who was now crying loudly, though without tears, swaggered from the café. He wanted to run but had been noticed too much already. Once outside, he crossed the road and when it was certain he was out of sight of any window watchers back in McDonald's he jogged towards the nearest bus stop.

Where was Jay?

Chapter 22

Kate sat at her desk pressing a cold cloth against her cheek. "I'll be fine. I'll see to it when I get home. My mouth is better already." She had tried to smile, mostly to reassure Dan Price who stood beside her with a cup of ice chips from the canteen. "Honestly, I've had worse." She didn't know how bad it was because she had avoided mirrors and window reflections. She was wobbly and shocked, and long experience both in the job and raising her family had taught her that seeing the damage before you were ready wasn't always helpful.

Tanya was in Bob Scunthorpe's office explaining just what had happened and how come yet another of her team had been hurt. He had come earlier to the office to talk to Kate and tried to send her home. She refused point blank to go to the hospital and had agreed to see the on-site nurse because it was the only way she could make him leave her alone: "We're short staffed, sir. We need to find this boy. We need all the bums on seats we can manage. I'm fine, I didn't bang my head or anything."

She knew when she went home her husband would be livid and her teenaged daughters would be horrified by her damaged face but right now, as far as she was concerned, the only way forward was to find the little shit who had done this. Apart from the assault on a police officer, there was the bigger and arguably more important issue of why he was in the house in the first place.

CCTV had been gathered from the area all around and now anyone who could find a seat in front of a screen was watching for the dark figure running from the house. They had picked him up on a camera outside a church at the end of the road. There was a huge breakthrough when he was caught on a bus camera and then followed through the town centre and finally seen entering McDonald's. Before they could act, they saw him leave. By the time Tanya joined them they were scanning buses leaving the stop in Cornmarket Street and there was an air of excitement in the room, everyone wanted to be the one who spotted him next.

"Are you okay, Kate?" Tanya grimaced when she saw the bruise darkening the other woman's face, the split lip which had started to bleed again and the developing shiner that had discoloured the white of her eye. "It looks sore."

"It's not so bad actually and the ice is helping. Anyway, what's the plan?" Kate said.

Tanya glanced around the room. "I know it makes sense to wait until we find out which bus he caught and where he went afterwards. In the meantime, though, I want Dan Price to go down to McDonald's, see if they remember him. They might be able to give us a decent description. Up to now he's been clever, hood up, face down. We need a better idea of what he looks like." She had included Dan in the conversation and by the time Tanya finished speaking he had his jacket on. "Take Detective Harris with you and, for God's sake, come back in one piece." The comment caused a ripple of laughter and it was good to feel the temporary lifting of the gloom. It would be back, they all knew. There was a funeral to attend and loss of one of their own to process but for the moment there was progress and the buzz was back.

Tanya took a seat alongside one of the civilians and began scanning camera footage. There were a few sideways glances, a few raised eyebrows but she didn't care. She wanted this boy and she wanted him quickly.

One of the civilians waved her hand in the air. "I've got him alighting in Castle Street, Detective Inspector. He went into the Westgate centre, north entrance."

"Get a car there, quick as you can. Kate, can you stay here and manage things, call the centre security. Have them post people at the entrances, give them what we have as a description. The rest of you monitoring live cams, keep your eyes open. If he gets out of there before I arrive, I want to know where he's gone."

She glanced around the room for someone to go with her. No Sue, Kate incapacitated, the two men already on their way to McDonald's. That had been a misjudgement but now there was no option but to go on her own.

"Detective Lewis, let the uniforms on site know I'm on my way." She ran from the room and down the corridor. This wasn't going off on her own. Well, it was, but what choice did she have? Anyway, it was just a young lad and there were going to be officers on the spot when she arrived. But this wasn't what Bob Scunthorpe had meant when he told her to keep out of trouble.

She flicked on her blue lights and screamed out of the car park, horn blaring.

Kate was on the Airwave urging cars to the town centre. It was mainly pedestrianised. She heard Kate speaking to cycle-mounted officers. The description of the boy was so vague. Jeans, a hoody, a backpack. No distinguishing marks on his clothes, nothing to make him stand out. It was as if he was deliberately dressed to be unnoticed.

A CSI team were back at the house, upstairs, looking for DNA and prints but it would be pure luck if he was on the system.

She activated the radio. "Detective Lewis, anything?"

"Not yet, ma'am. We've got officers there now; centre security guards are stationed at all entrances. He hasn't left."

"Okay, I'm nearly there. Keep me updated." Tanya had wanted to get the momentum back. Now, it was back. What they needed was a mixture of luck and good judgement. Surely, he couldn't give them the slip, not with the numbers on the ground. One kid – they had him. It was hard to see him as a murderer, but you just never knew. All they needed was to grab the little sod, that was all.

Chapter 23

Carl threaded his way through the crowd of shoppers. Instead of hanging around near the stairs or pacing along the aisles like wannabe cops with stab vests and radios, the security men moved with purpose towards the entrances to the centre. The hairs on the back of his neck had risen, he didn't know why, some sort of sixth sense. Then he heard the sirens outside and felt the change in atmosphere. A few mums gathered up their little kids and scurried out.

Perhaps he should get out, maybe there was something going on. He couldn't afford to be noticed because those women had very possibly reported him to the police. He wondered who they were. Cleaners maybe or estate agents. It occurred to him they could have been police. But they were just two women and they weren't in uniform. Why would the police come back to the house? He knew he'd clobbered one with his bag, he could get into trouble for that if they found him. The cops parked down the end of the street had reacted when the women started yelling. There was no doubt. Yes, perhaps they were police.

Still, he'd given them the slip, hadn't he? He'd kept his head down and now he was just part of the crowd. Things had calmed down, although there were plenty of police walking around. They weren't evacuating the centre so probably no need to panic. Be a good idea to change his clothes. He slipped into Primark. It was still busy in here. Women with babies, young girls rattling through the racks of tops and jeans, all oblivious to the atmosphere outside. He picked up a duffle coat, it was unlike anything he'd be seen dead in. Dorky and naff. He carried it around for a while slung over his arm. He picked up some jeans and draped them over the top. With a quick glance around he slipped into the changing rooms, pulled out his Swiss Army knife and cut off the tags with the little scissors. He pulled the coat on over his own jacket which was a good one not like the shop's cheap tat.

The two together made him look bulkier – that was good. The jeans were a bit long, but it didn't matter that they gathered over his trainers. He left the coat unbuttoned, casual-looking, and strolled back to the rack of jeans and threaded his old trousers onto an empty hanger. The next thing was a knitted hat from a display, and he cut the tag away. He made a small hole in the edge; the threads split and began to unravel as he dragged it on to his head, it looked old and worn. Nobody was going to look at him very closely. He dumped the tags on a shelf behind a pile of T-shirts and, stopping now and then, looking at the prices on jeans, picking up a T-shirt and then replacing it, he was careful not to glance back. They'd done this before, him and Jay, many times; why pay when you could just take what you wanted? He made his way to the door where a group of students was leaving, pushing and jostling. He latched onto them strolling alongside until they went into the nearby Pret. He walked along the South Arcade and out down the escalators. There was a security guard and a cop near the exit to Turn Again Lane and Carl squared his shoulders and marched past. He felt the blokes watching him. He stopped and pretended to check his phone, bent and re-tied his shoelace. The bravado worked and he was left alone.

Oxford city is one of the worst places in the country for bicycle theft and yet another badly secured two-wheeler, incorrectly tethered to the metal racks outside the centre, joined the numbers of missing bikes for the week. It was years since Carl had been on a bike, but it was like they said: you never forgot how to do it. The city was, as always, awash with people on bikes and in his new coat he blended right in with the students who were everywhere. The bus station was only a couple of minutes away and well signposted. It felt as though things were starting to go his way at last. He dumped the bike and draped the cheap duffle over the handlebars. He bought a sandwich and a Coke from the coffee shop, a ticket from the machine, and clambered aboard the bus to Birmingham. He had considered London for a while, but it was too far, too strange, too scary. He needed familiarity. He wanted home.

There was a seat next to the window near the back. With his feet up on the seat in front of him and his back hunched towards the aisle he knew he looked unfriendly. He put his bag on the seat and nobody tried to sit beside him. There were charging points on the bus and once there was enough juice, he opened the text signed 'G' and stared at it. He didn't know what to do. It was just as threatening as the first time he'd seen it. He wanted to delete it but couldn't summon up the courage. He tried Kayleigh's number again. It just went to voice mail. He didn't leave a message. He tried ringing his mum at home but there was no answer and she wasn't allowed to use her mobile phone while she was working. He sent her a message asking if Kayleigh had arrived home safely last night. She'd get it when she had her break.

The rocking of the big vehicle, the stuffy air and the drone of the engine lulled him and, although he struggled to stay awake, his head jerking painfully every few minutes, in the end his eyes closed and he drifted into sleep.

They were driving up the M40 when his phone vibrated and woke him. Rubbing at his eyes he peered at the screen.

An image had come into his WhatsApp feed. He clicked it open.

At first, he didn't understand what he was seeing. He enlarged the image. Kayleigh was looking out at him. Her eyes were huge, there were tears on her face. Her newly coloured hair was dishevelled and tangled. Her cheeks were streaked with runs of mascara. She was terrified, he could see. Behind her was a concrete block wall and it was dark where she was. It wasn't home and it wasn't Tracey's house. He was bolt upright now in his seat staring at the picture of his sister. He glanced around, there was no-one to tell, no-one to help.

The app chimed again. A message: *'We need to talk'*.

Chapter 24

Tanya paced back and forth across the office. She slammed a couple of chairs out of the way, picked up an empty takeaway cup and flung it towards the bin where it bounced from the rim, splashing cold coffee across the tiles. The team glanced at each other, pulled faces, and looked down at their hands.

"I do not believe this. How the hell can he have got out of there? How many bloody people were watching, how many uniforms were on site and none of you, not one of you saw him? It's a kid, just one kid and he's bested all of us," she said.

"Right, I want him found. We're going to go through the CCTV footage until we find him. He was there, we saw him go in, he didn't bloody well melt, he wasn't beamed up. I want him found, and quickly. I have to go and speak to DCI Scunthorpe now and tell him how the hell, with all the troops at our disposal, with cars and uniforms swarming around the place and with all of you staring at your screens we managed to lose this kid."

She stormed from the room and left the door to swing closed behind her. She wanted to slam it but knew from the past the damper precluded that expression of anger and just made you look stupid and feel furious. There was no sound, just a tense silence and the thud of her heels on the floor.

Brian Finch was sitting at the second desk in their shared office. He knew what had happened, of course he did. He nodded at her, he didn't go so far as to smirk, but she felt him judging her, gloating. It was in the tilt of his head, the twitch of his eyebrows, the way he didn't look away but waited for her to speak. She didn't give him the satisfaction. She sat at her desk and booted up her computer.

"Okay, Tanya. Anything I can do?"

Sod the man.

"No. Thank you. What have you found about detective Rollinson-Bakshi? Anything we weren't expecting?"

"I've viewed the footage – it's been enhanced, but I don't think we're going to find anything other than we already know. She was sent down to talk to them. But you know that." He shrugged. "I suppose it was just her bad luck."

Sod the bloody man.

"I've got a minute. Can I just have a look at the enhanced images?"

He glared at her. "I've pretty well finished with it to be honest."

Tanya pulled a chair up beside him. "If you would."

With a sigh he slid the line on the toolbar backwards. The images flickered in reverse. "So, we see Sue. She is talking to a workman on the ground at first."

"Yes, George he was called. He told her to speak to one of the others."

"Well, he walked away and left her on her own." He pointed at his screen.

"She turns and looks up," Finch said.

"Yes."

"It's only a short while later the stuff falls. You don't want to see, do you? It pretty grim."

"No, no leave it. I'll watch." Tanya leaned in closer.

Planks of wood and other building equipment filled the screen. For a moment Sue was frozen in horror and then she was under the debris. "Shit." Tanya couldn't hold back the expletive.

"Yes, I know. So, there we have it."

"Play the last bit again, Brian."

He sighed and made a show of gritting his teeth but did as she asked.

"What is she looking at?" Tanya said.

"She's just looking around, checking things out," Brian said.

Tanya stretched out a finger. "No, look. She's speaking."

"I don't think so. She's just checking."

"I'm not convinced. It's not clear enough but, to me, it looks as though there could have been someone up there on the scaffolding."

"What are you saying here? I thought it was not much more than an exercise so we could tell her family we'd been thorough."

"Yes, I know but it's more. We do have to make it count. I'm not happy."

"Tanya, I want to just put it to bed, let her family know it was what we first thought, a horrible accident. We were told there was no-one there, we can't see anyone. I'd be much better employed helping you with the actual murder. Perhaps you're looking for something to explain it, something so it makes more sense."

She ignored the final comment. "Brian, I reckon there could have been someone up there. If there was, who was it and why haven't they come forward and given evidence?"

He was silent for a minute, tapping at his teeth with the end of a pen. "Did you speak to the other bloke?"

"Which one?" Tanya asked. "Oh, you mean… Oh, bloody hell, what was his name? Steve was it, no – Stewart,

Stewart something. I didn't have a chance to speak to him myself when it happened, but somebody should have done, before he left the site. Find out."

"I don't remember seeing a statement from him. I'll follow it up. Maybe you do have a point. At the end of the day, she shouldn't have been able to stand where she was. No matter why she was there." He glanced at Tanya. "She shouldn't have been able to get access. Maybe that was his responsibility. Perhaps he thinks the company could be liable, maybe he's trying to protect them. I'll follow up on that but then, I think we've done all we can."

The change of focus had calmed her. "Keep me updated will you, Brian?"

"Yeah. And if you need any help chasing that young kid, you know I can step in."

She grabbed her bag and stomped down the corridor. Bob Scunthorpe was not going to be a happy bunny. Damn it, she was furious herself. Paul and Dan were walking the other way. Dan's smile of greeting froze as she approached. "I'll catch up later," she said. "In the meantime, get in the incident room and give them as much as you can about that bloody kid. Did you get a description?"

"Well, a bit of one yes, they noticed him because–"

"No time, go and tell those numpties in there and then get on the screens. We had him, bloody had him and then lost him and we shouldn't have done." She didn't wait for a response.

Chapter 25

Carl began to dial Kayleigh's number, again. Twice before he went as far as clicking the connect button and then disconnected before the call went through. The phone shook in his hand as his fingers trembled. He could feel sweat on his back, clammy and cold. They had heard stuff, him and Jay – stories about people vanishing – having accidents. One of the lads they had met had died, but it was an overdose. Everyone said he had taken some bad stuff and he was on his own in a play park. Nobody around to see him, to help him. They found him sprawled over the roundabout, his kit still there beside him. They had shrugged it off and refused to belief the rumours that he had crossed Gregor and had been killed as a warning. Anyway, even if it were true it was probably his own fault. That wasn't the sort of thing that would happen to them. They were too smart, too switched on and careful. All you had to do was make sure you turned in all the money and that the drugs arrived as and when you'd been told.

That was it, though, wasn't it? He hadn't taken the money back. It wasn't there – he hadn't had a chance. But Gregor wouldn't want to hear excuses. This was all the fault of that stupid old woman. Okay, she was dead, but that meant she didn't need to worry about anything. She was old anyway, what difference did it make to anyone. Old and on her own, and now the cause of all this hassle. Stupid bitch. She hadn't had to do anything. Just hold the stuff and then hold the money. Nothing more than opening the door and minding her own business.

Now, here it was. Jay had vanished and Kayleigh was in deep trouble. He knew he had to do something, but really it was Jay who had always made the decisions. He was older, more streetwise – he'd been doing this stuff for longer. His mother would be no use. He couldn't even call her. She'd just go to pieces and probably do something stupid. He couldn't call Granny. Granny didn't know he'd stopped going to school. There was no-one else. The kids he had been at school with, Johnny and Mo, he'd lost touch with them months ago now. They were still there, wearing the uniform, toting the bags of books, doing homework. It was another world, a world no longer available to him. He hadn't enjoyed school, but he hadn't hated it either. He'd done okay, got decent grades and he'd been good at sports. For a while there had been talk of college and a career. Stupid, he wouldn't have been able to do any of that stuff. There wouldn't have been money for further education or training. His dad just had his new family, he couldn't remember the last time he spoke to him. He couldn't help, wouldn't help. Carl shook his head. It was all gone now, school, his dad, any talk of college. His mother had ruined it all.

It was only supposed to be one time. Just one time taking a package for Gregor and then his mum would be clear. It might have been, should have been, but she had gone back again, couldn't keep away from the blow and the pills, so there was another package, another trip and then another. Then Gregor had paid him, a little roll of notes. He'd bought a new phone. Then there was another package, another payment and he was in. He hadn't known up to then that Jay was in it as well. They hadn't been close friends in school, but Gregor had sent them off together and they gelled. Both of them bandits, cool. They had money to spend, no more carting bags of books. Why bother to do that when there was money to be had for just riding round on trains and sitting in Maccy D's late at night, like gangsters. He had convinced himself it would last. It became more than just his mum. The origins were lost in the thrill and the money. They had planned. They would make themselves irreplaceable. They watched the men around Gregor, the ones with the dark glasses and the Rolex watches. They wanted some of that. All they had to do was toe the line and do what was asked of them.

Now though he was on his own. Kayleigh was in trouble and he had no-one to turn to. He was in deep shit. There was a lump in his throat and his eyes stung with tears. Well, okay – time to man up. Time to take charge. He gulped away the fear, knuckled his stupid eyes, turned off the caller ID and dialled Kayleigh's number.

There was silence when the phone was answered. Maybe the sound of breathing.

"It's Carl."

Whoever answered, it wasn't Gregor's voice. One of the others, then. One of the Rolex men. "Gregor wants to see you. Your sister wants to see you. You should hurry. You need to come today, in the next hour."

"I can't. I can't do that – I'm on the bus. I've been to Oxford. Tell Gregor, tell him I've been trying to sort things out. I've been trying to fix things. Tell my sister I'll be there – soon as I can. Tell Jayden, I've been trying to sort things out. Will you?"

"Jayden. You don't need to think about Jayden. Just your sister. You need to think about her. Forget Jayden now. You should hurry. Come to the unit."

The phone went dead.

Chapter 26

Bob Scunthorpe's desk was clear of all paperwork. He had a couple of files in a tray and his Mont Blanc pen on the blotter in front of him. He was in uniform. Tanya was struck, as she had been on other occasions, by his appearance. In his late forties or maybe early fifties, he had short hair, pepper-and-salt now but thick and well cut. He wore rimless glasses. His face was slightly tanned even after the winter. As far as she knew he didn't play golf, the middle-aged pastime of so many senior officers, but there were pictures in his office of himself and his family with their bikes. A couple of cycle racing trophies were pushed to the corner of his bookshelf. He was a handsome man and looked fit and vigorous. He also looked annoyed.

He nodded at her. He didn't invite her to sit. "I have been to see Sue Rollinson-Bakshi's family."

Well, that accounted for the uniform at least.

"Sir. They are lovely people. Her mother is very dignified," Tanya said.

"Indeed. I have told them, if they wish, Sue can have a force funeral, uniforms, an escort, flag and what have you. They haven't decided yet and I have given her my assurance we will honour their wishes but her close colleagues will attend no matter what."

"Yes, sir. Of course."

"Brian still has to get back to me with his final findings on her accident. I am not expecting any surprises, but I need to be able to tell her mother, in all honesty, we have done everything we can to find out what happened. The Health and Safety team have promised a report by early next week. The builder's investigation team are proving a little slower but I'm chasing them up. I had my doubts about tasking Brian with this, given the current workload. But in retrospect I think it was a good move on your part." He gave her a wry glance. "No matter what your true motives were." His mouth curled in a small smile.

Should she tell him now? What did she really know? Just that she wasn't totally happy. Tanya decided it would simply complicate things. She kept her mouth shut.

"Now, Detective Lewis?" He waited for an answer.

"Yes, sir. She insists she's okay and wants to continue working."

"Okay but I want her to see the nurse again on Monday. It's not looking good, is it, Tanya? We haven't moved on very far with the inquiry and you have a death and a nasty injury to show for it."

"Sir."

"We need some progress. I'm getting questions from higher up."

"We are looking for the youth who injured Detective Lewis. We don't know, at this point, what connection he has with Mrs Barker, but he was in the house, so the assumption has to be he is implicated in some way in the murder."

"And yet you lost him in the city centre."

"Yes, sir. We did."

"Not good enough, is it?"

Tanya didn't answer. She knew he was right and it made her embarrassed and angry. She wanted to look away, to stare at her feet but she kept her head up and her gaze steady. He nodded.

"Bring me something, Detective Inspector, and quickly."

"Sir."

He lifted one of the files onto the desk in front of him. She nodded, though he was no longer watching her, and she left, closing the door quietly behind her.

* * *

Back in the incident room she waited until she had everyone's attention. "Right, that was fun. Not. DCI Scunthorpe wants results. I want results. There is a pregnant woman in Australia who wants results so get your fingers out. Find me this boy. I expect you will all want to stay late tonight and come in over the weekend if necessary. Yes?"

There was a murmur of assent.

"So, where are we at?"

Dan Price stood up. He coughed quietly. Still shy despite his increasing familiarity with the team, he tried to avoid drawing attention to himself. The side effect of that was when he did take the floor, everyone listened. "It's probably only a small thing, boss. But I think, well, I reckon, I've seen the boy before. I've been conferring with Detective Lewis and she agrees with me."

"Yes, boss. I feel stupid I didn't see it before but with this…" She pointed to her discoloured face.

"So, come on." Tanya said.

"I am pretty sure he is one of two lads we saw on our first visit to the murder scene. I drove through a puddle. Soaked them. We thought they were just bystanders trying to get some pictures to flog. They scarpered pretty quickly but I think I recognise the jacket on the smaller one and his hair, his build, general appearance."

"Right. So, what have you done about it?"

"We've gone back to the CCTV from the day of the murder. We've been viewing film from all over the area and we think we've traced them. They ran off but we have been able to follow them and pick them up later boarding the train to Birmingham. I hope it's okay, boss. I've had a few people helping me. I've requested footage from Birmingham New Street station, whatever the new name is."

"Grand Central, Detective."

Dan waved a hand vaguely in the direction of a group of civilian workers and a couple of uniform officers who had volunteered to help. "Yeah, that's it. Thanks."

"Of course, I don't mind. Well done, Dan." She ignored the blush that had crept up his face and the regulations about physical contact and slapped him on the back, leaving her hand to lay on his shoulder for a moment. "Okay. Keep on it. As much information as you can. Excellent." She spun around to where Kate was sitting with her head in her hands. "Detective Lewis, please go home. You look bloody awful. Come back in tomorrow if you like but go home now. Get some arnica or whatever other gunk there is for bruises and take a couple of painkillers."

"Now, Dan, show me this little sod."

Chapter 27

It was raining again and overcast by the time Carl arrived at the unit, a small building on an industrial estate outside the city centre. The small warehouses were widely spaced and there wasn't a lot of activity; being Saturday most of the other prefabricated buildings were empty and shut down. The gates were padlocked and the parking spaces, behind wire fences, were empty. Gregor's unit looked abandoned. There were weeds growing through the cracked tarmac and puddles in the yard. Carl pushed the metal gate and it juddered open. He moved quietly through the empty space. The gloomy corners freaked him out a bit, but he reminded himself they didn't know exactly where he was. Jay had always said they tracked their phones and he wasn't sure whether it was true or not.

He didn't know what they used this place for, and he'd only been here once before. He'd waited outside while Jayden had gone inside, coming out with packages. That had been months ago now and they had never been back. They had picked up their stuff in many different places: houses, shops, even car parks. Wherever they had been told to go, they had gone, and now here he was once again because he had been told to. He was nothing more than a trained dog, he felt a spurt of anger and frustration.

The cars were at the back. Four of them tucked in a line along the back fence. Though the windows were covered with blinds a small leak of light confirmed someone was there. He glanced around. The place was deserted except for whoever was inside. He didn't know which car was Gregor's, he had never been in any of them. Maybe he changed, like the American president. Perhaps he was just driven in whichever one was available. There was so much he didn't know.

Where was Jay now? Maybe he was inside. He knew they were in trouble but perhaps Gregor had got them both down here. Jay might be inside and that would be brilliant. Together they could explain. What about Kayleigh. Was she in there? She'd be scared shitless if she was. Well, it was all going to be okay now. He'd go in and they'd sort it all out and he'd take Kayleigh home. He'd make his mum go to the doctor and then they'd get her off the stuff. Once she was clean, he'd get free of Gregor. He might even go back to school. Try it at least. He hadn't been excluded. It had been his choice to stop going so they couldn't stop him if he wanted to go back.

First, he'd go and see Gregor.

He knocked on the metal door and waited. There came the sound of shoes on gravel.

He stepped backwards and leaned to peer down the side of the unit. It was a narrow passage; he could see the shape of drainpipes. There were a few boxes discarded in the space and the rhythmic drip of water. He stepped forward and startled a cat that had been hunched and staring at something in the weedy edge. Rats probably. He pulled back. Rats could bite, and they carried the plague, he remembered that from history.

A car swept past on the road and as the noise receded the quiet was worse, spookier. *Sod this.* He kicked out at the bottom of the door. "Hey. It's me, Carl. I'm waiting outside. Come on, man. Let me in – I'm freezing my balls off and it's starting to rain again."

He felt disturbance in the air around him, heard the crunch of footsteps. Fast and close. He whirled around. The bloke was big, he was inches away. Carl heard him laugh, just one puff of humour. The bag was over his head in seconds. Before he had time to react. He dropped his phone and clawed at the sacking. The big bloke dragged it downwards so now it was over his shoulders and his upper arms. The blow on the side of his head, when it came, was enough to knock him to the floor and he heard another laugh. He kicked out with his legs but there was nothing there to connect with. The other man could see, he could move. Carl could not.

They dragged him to his feet and pushed him forward, stumbling and staggering. He heard the door open and felt the change in air. There were two of them now, one on each side and they manhandled him onto a hard seat. There was light beyond the sacking. A smell of tobacco.

They didn't tie his hands; he had expected them to but kept them still, didn't want to draw attention in case it was an oversight. The low mumble of voices stilled, and he tensed, waiting for what was to come next.

Chapter 28

An interview with Carol Barker's daughter was arranged for early on Saturday morning. It could be tricky. There was nothing much to tell her and yet there were some difficult questions. Either the woman would be embarrassed and admit to youthful indiscretion or practically anything from outright denial to confusion regarding the drug residue.

Tanya was tired and fed up but, as always, arriving home to her warm house cheered her. The lights had come on automatically, the flame effect fire cosied the living room and her music was already playing. The outlay to automate her home had been expensive and she was only just getting used to it but tonight she appreciated the 'internet of things'.

Mrs Green, the cleaner, had been a bit sniffy about it all. "I can turn the lights on before I leave, and you can put the music player on a timer thing."

"Yes, I know but this is personalised, and I can do it remotely." Tanya had said. The response had been a quiet tut as the woman left.

Alexa couldn't polish the furniture though or water the plants and change the bedding. Not yet. So, Mrs Green was safe for a fair while longer.

Tanya picked up the mail and the parcel from the table in the hall. It was her new summer jacket probably. There was a post card from her sister, on holiday in Portugal with the kids, and a letter from the bank. She recognised the return address immediately and her good mood threatened to dissolve. She threw the envelope onto the counter in the kitchen and poured a glass of wine. She'd deal with it later. For now, she wanted to look at the new blazer and have a few minutes to herself before she opened her computer and started on the report for the day.

The phone rang just as she kicked off her shoes.

"Boss, it's DC Price."

"Hello, Dan. What's happening?"

"We've had some luck with the British Transport Police in Birmingham. They reckon they know our youth."

"Brilliant – what do we know?"

"They've had him a couple of times for fare avoidance. I'm expecting details in the next few minutes. I'll forward them to you."

"Is there an address."

"Yes, boss. Do you want it now? It's in Birmingham."

"Okay." She scribbled down the details and clicked on Google Earth, zooming in on the row of small brick houses. "I suppose it makes more sense to wait until tomorrow. Meet me at the office. No, wait, I'll pick you up about seven in the morning. Oh shit – I've got that call to Australia. Look, leave it with me. I'll sort something. At the moment the plan is to go to his home address early tomorrow. Excellent work, Dan, really great."

She grabbed her laptop and took it through to the kitchen where her glass of wine was waiting. She'd email Kate to do the call. Then she remembered it would be Skype and Kate's face would hardly be reassuring, bruised and battered as it was. Paul Harris wasn't the right one to speak to a vulnerable and grieving woman. She called Dan back. "Change of plan, Detective. I want you to question Mrs Barker's daughter tomorrow. We need to know if the drug residue was anything to do with her. She might be up front but if not, we'll have to rely on your impression of her response. Can you handle it?"

"I can, ma'am."

"Good man."

When she called Kate, the woman was insistent she was ready and able to make the trip to Birmingham. "I'll let DCI Scunthorpe know and ask him to liaise with Snow Hill. I need to leave Dan Price here to hold the fort. We need help but the only other body, Brian, is busy with Sue's accident and anyway I don't want him involved in my case," Tanya said.

"It's fine, boss. I feel okay. I look a mess, but I feel fine."

"How did your husband and the girls take it?"

"Oh, you know. A bit upset. They've been spoiling me though, so that's nice."

Tanya didn't know. There wasn't ever anyone to bother if she came home with bumps and bruises, though Charlie Lambert always expressed concern when she got herself knocked about. He still remembered working with her and saving her life at least once. But Charlie was up on Merseyside, so her injuries were always just her concern. She told herself she wouldn't want the hassle of someone fussing over her, but it might be nice now and then. Ah well, it was what it was. The main thing right now, though, was there was movement. Something to work with, something to report. Almost unthinkingly, she tore open the white envelope on the counter and dragged out the paper. Still overdrawn, almost to the limit, still maxed out on her credit card and now they were refusing to honour the Direct Debit for her council tax payment. They *suggested* she make an appointment with the debt advisor at her earliest convenience.

Yeah, yeah, she would. Once this boy was found and she'd solved just what happened in Summertown leaving a decent woman bleeding to death in the rain. She stuffed the envelope into the kitchen drawer with several others.

Chapter 29

When Tanya picked up Kate, she saw George, her husband, watching from the bedroom window. As she opened the car door Kate turned and waved up at him.

"He's in a bit of a strop with me," she told Tanya. "He wanted me to take time off. He knows we're short of officers but when it comes down to me social conscience gets a bit kicked backwards."

"How long have you been married?" Tanya asked.

"Nearly twenty-five years."

"Wow. That's long."

"Yeah, well, what can I tell you? I was a child bride of course." Kate grinned. She flicked down the sun visor to examine her face in the integral mirror. "I tried make-up before I left, but it just made it look worse."

"It's a bit of a mess, isn't it?" Tanya said.

"Oh thanks, boss. That makes me feel a lot better."

"Sorry. I just meant – it looks sore, still swollen."

The other woman turned and laughed. "It's okay, really. I've had worse and at least he didn't break any teeth. I just worry it could upset people."

"Well, if this lad is who we think he is, he needs to be upset. If nothing else, we can have him for assault on a police officer."

"Hmm."

"What, don't you want the little sod punished?"

"Let's just wait, eh. Let's find out what's going on with him. From the images I've seen he's pretty young. Doesn't even look as though he's left school yet."

"No, I know, but that doesn't excuse him belting you with a backpack. Anyway, I suppose the main thing is what the hell was he doing in that house. Not meaning to minimise that…" Tanya pointed to Kate's face. "But if he was there, he could very likely have had something to do with the murder. I can't believe he just thought he'd break in because it was empty, can you?"

"No, probably not. Still, let's see what he has to say for himself. He was obviously scared stupid, and he might not have known we were police."

"Doesn't excuse him though."

Kate obviously wanted to change the subject. "What do you reckon about the drug residue then, boss? A bit weird, isn't it? I mean, she was quite an old woman, our vic."

"Yeah, she was but she had contact with youngsters, didn't she?"

"What are you suggesting? She was dealing?" Kate had turned to stare at Tanya, her eyes wide, eyebrows disappearing into her fringe.

Tanya shrugged. "I wouldn't say I was suggesting it exactly. It's just a possibility."

"But the parents we have spoken to, the neighbours – nobody has said anything other than she was a nice woman and a good teacher."

"Yes, I know, but really how well did they know her?"

"True – but her daughter said how much she liked kids, how committed she was."

"Yes, but her daughter hasn't lived with her for a while. Again, how much did she really know about her everyday life?"

"Nah. I can't see it. Jeez, I certainly hope not anyway. That's horrible."

"Well… drugs. That whole world is horrible, isn't it?"

Kate puffed out her lips and shook her head. "It'd be like my mum being a dealer."

"Not impossible though, is it? Oh sorry, I didn't mean your mum, obviously."

"No." Kate laughed. "Still, old people, young kids – this is like a plague."

"Yes. I think that's a good description. You remember what happened to my niece. It was all because of drugs in the end, wasn't it? And, though she seems to be doing okay I do wonder what long-term damage has been done. Will it come back to haunt her – the rape – later? Maybe when she gets married, has kids of her own. We suppress a lot, don't we? PTSD can get you much later when you think you're over something."

Kate waited in silence. But Tanya stopped talking and after a while she turned on some music and there was just the quiet hum in the background, occasionally interrupted by the sat nav as they sped on up the motorway.

Kate closed her eyes and leaned back into the seat. "Is it okay if I close my eyes for a bit? My head's pounding. I took painkillers before I left the house, but they haven't kicked in yet. George wanted me to stay in bed, to bring me breakfast. It would have been nice but…" She shrugged. "I couldn't let the team down."

Shortage of manpower had far-reaching effects, not least robbing Kate of the pampering by her family when she could really have done with it. Tanya glanced across the car and turned down the music.

Chapter 30

The warble of Tanya's phone woke Kate and she grabbed out to answer it without thinking. "Thanks, I've got it," Tanya said. But she smiled as she clicked the button to turn on the speaker. "Dan. You're on speaker. What have you got for us?"

"Hello, boss. Hiya, Kate, hope you're feeling better. So, I've completed the call with Stella Barker. She's in hospital, I'm afraid. Something to do with stress and the baby."

Beside her Tanya heard Kate sigh deeply.

"Anyway, we were able to use Skype and she was adamant she had never used drugs of any sort when she lived with her mum. Apparently, she was a dancer when she was younger and a bit of a fitness freak – sorry, not a freak – well, you know what I mean. Anyway, I believed her, and she was so sure her mum would never have anything to do with drugs. It was convincing. She didn't even drink much, and Stella was very clear her mother would do nothing to encourage her students down that route. Oh yes, apparently, she worked with the Samaritans for a while and knew all about the devastation addiction causes. Honestly, boss, I just can't see her dealing or indeed taking illegal substances. I suggested maybe the students themselves were hiding drugs in the house, but Stella Barker didn't buy that. Her mother was pretty strict about what access the kids had."

"Okay, thanks, Dan. Of course Stella won't want to think that her mum could be involved in anything dodgy. But it's a long time since she lived at home and probably Carol wouldn't want to worry her if she was having any trouble with the students, especially now she's pregnant. I don't think we can discount it totally but it's information anyway. Has there been any luck with the search for the weapon?"

"Nothing yet. Oh. Before you go, DI Finch wants a word, boss. He knows you are out this morning but would like a call when you're free."

"Okay, noted. Bye, Dan, keep me up to date with any developments. I want everyone concentrating on finding this lad."

* * *

"So, that doesn't help does it?" Kate said.

"Nope. I wonder if the kids brought it. You know, the older students she was teaching, and they hid it. After all it's a long time since Stella was there; things change, don't they?"

"Yes, that's got to be on the cards. Have we checked whether this lad we're looking for was actually a student?" Kate asked.

"I went through the list we have and the name the Transport Police gave us didn't show and she did seem to be pretty efficient about keeping records. I wonder why it all went wrong. She seemed to be switched on and then she stopped teaching and seems to have just shrunk into herself. Her GP didn't think she had dementia although she was depressed. It takes us back to drugs again, doesn't it? Could she have been taking them herself? At first it didn't seem likely but there has to be an explanation somewhere."

* * *

Carl's address was a narrow redbrick house which had seen better days. The curtains drooped limply at the windows and the flags in the small front garden were mossy and uneven. Litter had collected in the corners. Tanya tried the bell, but they didn't hear it chime inside so, after a short wait, resorted to hammering with the side of her fist.

There came the rattle of locks and when the door opened it was held closed by a chain. They held up their warrant cards and Tanya stepped forward, leaning into the narrow gap. "Mrs Grant?"

There was no answer. The pale thin woman narrowed her eyes at them, but she didn't speak.

"I wonder if we can come in and speak to you?" Tanya lifted her hand to push against the door. "It's about Carl. Is he here?"

"No. He's not here."

"Do you know where he is, Mrs Grant?" Kate asked.

"Why. What has the little sod done this time? If he's been shoplifting again, I don't want to know. I told him, no more."

"We just want a quick word. You have no idea where he is then? Look," – as she spoke Tanya pushed harder at the door – "why don't you let us in, and we can just have a quick chat. If you want to ask a neighbour in, that's okay."

"No, I don't want a neighbour in…" As she answered, Carl's mother screwed up her face and shifted her gaze back and forth as if the neighbours might be standing watching. The idea seemed to make up her mind and she unhooked the little chain and dragged open the door. The narrow hallway was dim and littered with shoes and bags. There were clothes piled on the bottom step, waiting to be taken upstairs. The skinny woman walked the length of the house and into the kitchen at the back. The air was murky with tobacco smoke but though there were a couple of mugs on the draining board the kitchen was tidy. A small

126

bunch of flowers was in a jug on the windowsill. Carl's mother sat on one of the wooden chairs at the kitchen table and dragged an ashtray towards her. She didn't invite her visitors to sit.

"So, can you tell us when you last spoke to your son?" Tanya asked.

"Couple of days ago I think."

"You think? You don't know?" Kate said.

"Well, he comes and goes as he pleases. I can't be after him all the time. He's grown up, nearly a man. You know what they're like. Him and his bloody sister. Don't give a damn about me, neither of them. She was supposed to be home now as well but she's off with her bloody mate. I might as well not have had kids."

"Have you got his mobile number?" As she asked the question, Kate pulled out another chair and sat across the table. She leaned in and Tanya was reminded again just how empathetic her colleague was. "We really do need to have a word with him."

"What's he done?"

"We don't know he's done anything yet. That's why we want to talk to him. Just to make sure he's okay."

A small black phone was rooted from the bottom of Frances Grant's bag and she flicked through her contact list. "There, that's him. I've tried to call him. I wanted to ask him if he knew where Kayleigh is. Neither of them answers." There was the glint of tears in the woman's eyes, but she gulped them away and picked up her cigarette.

As expected, there was no response to the attempt to call. "Get a trace organised, will you?" Tanya said.

"Hey. Just a minute, you can't. I didn't give it to you so you could do that. Leave him alone. Just leave him alone. You'll get him into trouble."

"How do you mean?" Kate asked.

The woman pressed her lips together. She glanced out of the window. "Nothing. I want you to go. Leave us alone. Just go. I don't want you here anymore."

It gave them no choice but to leave. Kate turned at the last minute. "We'll keep you informed, Mrs Grant, if you give us your number. We'll let you know when we find him."

"No, you're not having my number. When you find the little sod just tell him to bloody well call me. Tell that Jayden as well. His mum's been calling me over and over. They'll be together, they always are."

"Have you got Jayden's number?"

"No. I've got his mum's, though. Bloody woman won't leave me alone. If my boy's in trouble, it's Jayden's fault. He's the one you should be looking for." She handed over the handset and Kate copied the number.

"Where does he live, Jayden?" Tanya asked.

"Goldsmith Road. Just round the corner, the house two doors from the end. There'll be a blue car in the front, some big American thing – old. You can't miss it."

As they turned to leave, she stepped over the threshold. "Hey, if you find him. Tell him to call me, eh?"

Kate nodded and smiled at the woman. "Poor thing," she muttered as they walked down the short path. "She needs some help."

Tanya grunted in response.

Chapter 31

It was better when Kayleigh stopped crying. She was still sniffing now and then, and her breath came in sobs but at least the crying had stopped. When he first saw her, Carl was relieved. She wasn't tied to a chair or blindfolded. There were no bruises on her face, and she was, as far as he could tell anyway, fully dressed. But as soon as he walked into the cold room she had burst into tears. She leapt from her chair but when one of the men stepped forward, she sat again, grasping at the sides of the seat.

The blokes had laughed. One of them had taken hold of her face in his hands and squeezed her cheeks leaving dark red finger marks when he let her go.

"Carl." She didn't manage any more.

"It's alright, Kay. It's going to be fine now." One of Gregor's men had turned and sneered at him. "Be quiet, boy," he'd said.

"Where is Gregor?" Inside, Carl was shaking, his hands were quivering but he managed to keep his voice steady, to hold his head up. This guy was only the same as him after all, one of Gregor's minions. Just a gofer.

It was easy to convince himself with distance between them but when the man came closer to tower over him, his tobacco breath in his face and the smell of cologne strong in his nose, Carl felt his stomach lurch. He thought he might be sick.

"Not for you to ask the questions, little boy. You wait now. You and your sister will wait. Gregor will come when he has time. He is angry. You have his money."

"No, no I don't– I don't have any of his money."

"Then you better have his stuff."

"I don't– look, I need to tell him about it. I need to explain."

"Yes. Yes, you do." The burly thug laughed again, an unamused puff, more a grunt than anything. "You wait." With the final instruction he clapped his companion on the shoulder. "Stefan." Just one word and they turned and dragged Kayleigh upright. She screamed, her feet scuffling on the floor, twisting, and struggling.

"Leave her alone. Get off her." Carl threw himself across the narrow space between them but before he could do more than simply kick out and thump at the bloke's back, he was knocked to the floor by the one called Stefan. He rolled and leapt to his feet again. But it was too late, his sister was dragged across the room screeching and squirming.

They were never going to be any sort of match for the two big blokes. The room they were pushed into was little more than a cupboard. There was a light set in the ceiling behind a metal cage, the glass shade was full of tiny black bodies. There were metal shelves, but they were solid and immovable, the frame bolted to the floor.

When Stefan and his mate slammed the door, Kayleigh slid her back down the wall to sit with her head on her bent knees, keening. Carl knelt beside her. He tried to put his arm around her shoulder, but she shrugged him away, raising a sodden face to glare at him.

"Have you seen Jay?" Carl said.

"What?"

"Jay, have you seen Jayden while you've been here?"

"Jay, is that all you're bothered about? No, I haven't seen bloody Jayden. I haven't seen anybody except those two arseholes and Gregor. I don't believe you. I've been locked in here. I've been terrified and bullied and…" She stopped and Carl's heart jinked. "And all you can think about is your stupid mate. You don't give a shit about anyone but yourself."

"No, it's not that – honestly. It's just, to sort this out I need Jay to back me up. I need to explain what's happened to Gregor, and Jay was with me." Carl waited for a moment, he didn't want to ask the next question, he didn't want the answer that would colour his life forever, but he owed it to her. "Did they hurt you, Kayleigh?"

She held up an arm and showed him bruises, pulled back her hair to reveal more on her neck. "Did they bloody hurt me? What do you think these are?"

"No. No that's not what I mean. I mean did they do anything more to you. Shit, Kay, you know what I mean. Did they rape you?"

Her face softened as tears sprang to Carl's eyes and she shook her head. "No. They didn't. But they bloody terrified me, they laughed at me and it's no thanks to you that's all they did. This is all your fault, yours, and Jayden's."

"I know. I'm so sorry, Kayleigh. But I did try to warn you. I told you not to try and go home, I told you not to be on your own."

"Oh, right so it's my fault now. I've got to stay in, I've got to do what you say just because you and your stinking mate have screwed up. Shit, Carl. I'll never forgive you for this." She lowered her head and began to cry again.

"Don't, Kayleigh. Please don't. I'll fix this. I just need to talk to Gregor, and it'll be okay." He came closer and this time when he put his arm around her shoulders, she didn't shrug him away. She leaned against him and sighed. "I want to go home, Carl. I just want to go home. I want Mum."

"Listen." Carl held up his hand.

"What?"

"A phone. Can you hear a phone?"

Kayleigh tipped her head to one side, her brow furrowed as they listened. "I think so."

"It is. It's Jay's phone. Well, it's his ringtone anyway. He downloaded it. What are the chances one of those idiots would have the same one? He must be here. He must be here somewhere. "Jay! Jay! Can you hear me? Jay! It's Carl."

Chapter 32

Tanya knocked on the blue front door of the house with the vintage Pontiac parked outside.

They knocked and waited. The woman who answered was tall and broad. She wore a nurse's uniform and her hair was in tiny braids, they jigged and danced as she moved. Brown eyes twinkled but the look on her face was far from friendly. There was worry, and distrust, and impatience or maybe anger. "You come to tell me about my boy?" she asked. She took hold of Tanya's ID and flicked it over in her hand before handing it back.

"Your boy?"

"My Jay. He's been missing."

"How long has he been gone?" Kate said.

"Coupla days. I been calling him. Look, if you have to tell me hard news, you just do it."

"Maybe we could just come inside?" Kate said.

The woman sighed but she stood back then ushered them into her warm, tidy house. "Look, I know my boy is astray. I know he needs to get back on a righteous path but if he's in trouble I'm here for him. I am. If he's been hurt…" She stopped and passed a hand over her eyes. "Or if it's worse just tell me."

"We have no reason to believe your son is hurt, Ms erm…"

"Gormon. Lydie Gormon and it's Mrs, though the useless lump of a husband is long gone. My boy has got himself into a bad place. I know it. I have tried but he's nearly a man now and he sees what happens and it makes him angry. You know, young black men – in this country. It's not easy for them. He doesn't tell me what he's doing. I can't follow him, can't keep him in the way I did when he was little. I know it's wrong, just the way a mother knows. That's why I didn't call you. Police. I didn't want you having his name, didn't want him on any lists and what have you."

"Do you have any idea where he might be?" Tanya asked. She liked this woman and felt sorry for her. Though she had no idea what it must be like to be bringing up a teenaged boy, she remembered the anguish when her own niece disappeared just a year or so ago.

"No. He was with that Carl boy. They are always together. I hate to think what they might be up to. I rang his phone. I rang it over and over. One time there was an answer, but no-one spoke. There was someone there, but he didn't speak. Might have been my Jay, might not." She shrugged and flopped into the easy chair in front of the fireplace. For a minute she lowered her head into her hands and then with a deep breath she looked back at them. "Look, I don't know what he's up to. I don't know whether he's in trouble or not. But I want him home and I'll do whatever you want me to do to bring him back. He don't seem to have any more friends these days than Carl, and I don't know where he goes but if I can help you, I will."

"We want to trace his phone," Tanya said. The other woman nodded. "I assume he has a computer?"

"Oh yes, in his room. You want to look? You take it – whatever you want."

"Thank you, Mrs Gormon. It might be a great help. We want to find your boy, we want to find his friend but I feel it only fair to warn you if he has been involved in anything illegal we will have to look at that and if necessary take action."

"Yes, of course you will. I know. Maybe that's what it's going to take to get him back on the straight road. First though, get him back for me. Just bring him back and then I can deal with what comes. I've been out when I had the chance. Walking the streets, standing outside his school, the places he goes. I haven't had sight nor sound of him. I just want him back now."

They looked in Jayden's bedroom with his mother standing in the doorway, arms crossed, leaning against the door frame. When they found a small stash of weed in a box in the top of his wardrobe, she showed little surprise simply raising her eyebrows and shrugging. They took away his laptop but apart from the computer, there didn't appear to be very much to help.

"Thank you for your cooperation, Mrs Gormon, we appreciate it," Tanya said as she slid the computer into an evidence bag and filled in the label. "We'll get a trace out on his phone and I promise you as soon as we hear anything, we'll let you know. You have my card. If you hear from him or any of his friends or, if you think of anything that might help, please give me a call, anytime, anytime at all."

* * *

"They have to be up to something, don't they? First, down at the scene, then both of them going missing." As she spoke, Kate belted herself into the car and began to scroll through the messages on her phone.

"I think so. But it's interesting only Carl was at the house when we were there. When that happened." Tanya waved a hand in the direction of Kate's head.

"Yeah, it's true and it gives me a bad feeling. According to both women they are always together, they were together when Dan splashed them with the puddle and reading the report from the Transport Police," – she wagged her phone – "they are usually together when they've been picked up a couple of times for avoiding buying tickets. So, what has made them separate now? We know Carl is about somewhere but where the hell is his mate?"

"Can you contact DCI Scunthorpe for me, ask him to get in touch with Snow Hill and see if they have someone there to look at this computer? I reckon we should hang around for a while in case there's something on it and I don't want to compromise it if they have been involved in anything. We need the Cyber Crime Unit on this, and we need it done quickly. They may be guilty of something, they may not. But with them both being missing it could be they're in trouble themselves. If they are, we need to move fast."

Chapter 33

"Shut up, you moron." Kayleigh thumped Carl hard on the arm. "Stop yelling. You'll have those two back in here."

He ignored her and stood close to the door shouting his friend's name over and over. He rattled the metal shelving.

"Stop it. Bloody stop it, Carl. He's not here. He's not answering. Shut up."

"What do you mean he's not here? I heard his phone."

"Yeah, but can you hear it now?"

"No. But I heard it for sure." He rattled the door handle. "Jayden. Hey, can you hear me?"

The quiet when he stopped yelling was absolute. They stood together listening. Carl could hear the pound of blood in his ears and the in and out rasp of his own breath. He felt Kayleigh's thin fingers curl around his own and he turned to see tears trailing down her cheeks and dripping, unnoticed, onto the dirty floor. Seeing her now, frightened and beaten, tore him apart. He took a breath. Okay, he was the man here. She was his sister, his people, and it was his job to look after her. The knowledge she was only in this mess because of what he had done, what their mother had become, crawled into his mind. Well, okay then. His fault, his job to get her out of here and sort this. The trouble was he didn't have a clue how he was supposed to do it.

There were no windows in this little room. The door was solid, it didn't even rattle in the frame and it was obvious they were alone. All the noise he'd just been making would have brought the two goons back if they'd heard. Jayden wasn't there or wasn't able to help. Maybe he was there, and he had become one of them totally. Maybe he had gone over to the other side. He had always been impressed by Gregor. He had often said he intended to have all the things the big man had, no matter what. Perhaps he had dropped his friend right in the shit to impress the others. He pushed that aside for now. It was too scary and too sad.

"It's okay, Kayleigh. Once Gregor gets here, I'll be able to explain and then we'll go home. Some heavy shit has gone down but it's not all my fault."

"What's happened? Why is Gregor after you?"

"Aw, come on, Kay. You know I can't talk about that stuff with you. You know about Gregor and Mum. Well, let's just say she owed him, and I was paying him back. But now, well it's totally messed up."

"How though? How has it gone wrong?"

He spun away from her. "It just has. I'm not telling you. I don't want to talk about it. Me and Jay, we got into a situation. I don't want to talk about it. Just leave it, yeah?"

She opened her mouth to speak again but they heard the crash of the outer door, footsteps across the floor and then the rattle of the locks to their little room.

Carl rushed forward. He pushed his sister behind him and stood four-square to the door as it swung open. His fists were clenched at his side, his shoulders set and inside he was jelly.

Gregor filled the space. His height and bulk obscured most of the faint backlight. He ran his hand across his short brown hair and sighed.

"Come on out, boy!" He pointed at Kayleigh as she began to move. "No. You stay there. You wait." He turned and walked out into the bigger room. Carl squeezed Kayleigh's shoulders. "It's okay. It'll all be over in a bit now."

"Don't leave me, Carl." She sobbed.

"'course I won't. I promise." He heard her frightened gasp as Stefan slammed the door and turned the key.

Gregor was waiting. For a long minute he didn't speak. He nodded once and then lit up one of his cigarettes. "Where is my money?"

"I don't have it. Where's Jay? Has Jay not explained?"

"Don't worry about Jayden. He's gone now. You don't need to think about him anymore. Jayden is over."

"What do you mean? I don't understand. How is he over?"

Stefan had come up behind, quietly, and now his hand snaked around Carl's neck. He grabbed his fist with the other hand and pulled – hard. No matter how he clawed and dragged at the thick, muscular arm Carl couldn't move it, not at all. He couldn't breathe, couldn't speak. Stars filled his head, darkness threatened from the edges of his vision. His legs weakened. His body leaked strength and he felt himself sag and begin to fall.

Stefan released his grip, not much – the arm was still there with Carl hanging on. It was more to keep himself upright now than to try and pull it away. He gasped, drawing air into his aching lungs. Gregor leaned closer.

"Jayden is gone. You are here. Where is my money? You went to the house. My contacts told me the money was there, it had been left. Same as always. They had taken the supplies. Now, there was just you and the old woman. She's dead. I saw it on the news. So, why is she dead and where is my money?"

"I don't know. I truly don't."

"Don't lie to me boy. Jayden tried to lie. Don't make the same mistake."

"What did he tell you?"

"It doesn't matter. I want to know from you. Where is my money?"

"I don't know. We didn't get into the house. We went over the fence, the way we always do, and she was in the garden. The old woman was in the garden and she was lying under the tree and there was blood everywhere. We ran away. We didn't go into the house. I went back later when the police had gone."

Now Carl saw he could turn what he'd done since that night to his advantage – maybe.

"I went back, Gregor, to see. It wasn't there though. There was nothing there. I reckon the police must have it. They had pulled the place apart. I went back to try and find it but there was nothing there. Nothing in the hiding places."

Gregor scratched the side of his neck and sniffed. He turned to Stefan. "This is what the other boy said. But he didn't go back. Hmm, maybe after all it's true – shame. Okay – let him go. Put him back in the storeroom. Give him some water. I will decide later what to do with them."

"Gregor, this wasn't our fault. She was lying on the grass bleeding. We just ran away. I don't know what happened to her. Where's Jay?"

"Enough talk now. I told you Jayden is gone. Forget him."

When they pushed him back into the small room Kayleigh grabbed at him. Stefan threw two bottles of water onto the floor, turned, and locked the door. Carl ran to the corner and vomited against the wall, wet puke splashing his trainers and the bottoms of his jeans.

Chapter 34

"I've got a response from DCI Scunthorpe, boss." Kate held up her phone. "We need to see DCI Parker. He's lined up someone to take the laptop. Our own people are trying to get a trace on Jayden's number."

"Good. I remember DCI Parker from before. It wasn't all plain sailing between me and him, but he's a decent officer and just think – we sent him Brian Finch. He's got to love us for that."

"Ow." Kate lifted a hand to her mouth. "Don't. I can't smile, the split lip starts to leak again."

They parked at the station in the centre of Birmingham and were ushered straight through to the Cyber Crime Unit where a detective was waiting to take the computer. "What sort of thing am I looking for?" he asked.

"To be honest I'm not at all sure. Have you had a chance to go through the notes on this case?" Tanya said.

"I had a scan of it. What are you thinking? Drugs obviously, but what else? Are you considering child abuse?"

"How do you mean?" Tanya said.

"Well, they are minors, aren't they?"

"They are. But the victim is an old woman, decent from everything we've heard, and these are not young vulnerable kids. They are older teens and a couple of tearaways by all accounts."

"From what we see here all kids are vulnerable. You'd be surprised."

"Sorry, yes of course. The boy's mother seemed to think he was up to things he shouldn't be but couldn't give us any help as to what. Look, I'm just going to have to rely on your expertise and thanks so much for the help."

"Okay. I'll see what I can do. I suppose it's urgent. It's always urgent."

"We've got two boys and possibly a girl missing."

The tech guy reached to take the computer and wagged a form for Tanya to sign. He turned away and called back over his shoulder. "I'm on this. If anything pops, I'll let you know straight away."

Tanya turned to Kate. "I'll go up and speak to the DCI. Why don't you head down to the canteen and get a brew? I'll meet you there."

"Cool. I'll get you a drink. Do you want anything to eat?"

"I wouldn't mind a sandwich. Here, let me give you some money." It shamed Tanya that she was relieved when Kate waved a dismissive hand. She knew there was not enough in her purse to buy them both lunch and it would have been beyond embarrassing to only pay for herself. "My shout next time then," she said.

* * *

After her meeting with the DCI, Tanya joined Kate. There was another officer, a female in uniform at the table.

"Boss, this is Custody Sergeant Theresa Hill," Kate said.

"Please, call me Terry."

Tanya nodded as she unwrapped her sandwich.

"We've just been having a chat about a mutual acquaintance," Kate said.

"Oh, I don't think…" said Theresa.

"It's okay, Terry. DI Miller is one of the good guys. She's had quite a bit of experience with DI Finch."

"Still, though." The other woman shook her head. "Look I've got to get back. It was nice to meet you, Kate, and you, Detective Inspector."

They watched as she wove between the tables, deposited her tray, and disappeared through the double door.

"What was that about then?"

Kate thought for a moment. "I don't know now whether I should say anything. She obviously didn't want me to. Oh, what the hell, it'll come out soon anyway, forced to."

"What will?"

"Well, to put it in a nutshell, she's got an outstanding complaint under investigation against DI Finch."

"Really. What for, him being a dick or just generally an unpleasant know-all?"

"Well, kind of. For bullying and homophobic remarks. She didn't have time to tell me much. She was really nice, she came over to ask about my face, whether I needed any painkillers or anything."

Tanya looked back at the door. "Oh. Right. Is she–"

"Yeah. Married actually, to someone called Fliss. She showed me some wedding pictures."

"Ah. So, is that why we have him back with us?"

"Could be, boss. Could very well be. It's a bit of an eye opener, isn't it?"

"I'm not so sure how surprised we should be. Interesting though."

The conversation was interrupted by the chime of Tanya's phone. "Dan, what have you got?"

As she listened, she waved her hand towards the cups and sandwich wrappers, a 'collect them together' sort of wave. Kate picked up the message and ran to get a couple of go-cups from the counter.

By the time she was back Tanya was already on her feet. "We've got a location for Jayden's phone. Not far from here, apparently. I need to run up and organise some back up if I can. I'll meet you in the car. Take my coffee, will you?" She threw the car keys to Kate and they dashed from the canteen in opposite directions.

Chapter 35

"They've given us one patrol car with a couple of bods. Nothing else available right now. DCI Parker said if we think there is a 'situation' he'll do what he can. I don't know what three missing kids connected with a murder is if it's not a situation, but I suppose I understand his point. There might be nothing or we might just find these little tearaways smoking pot and drinking cider – do they still do that? – drink cider, I mean?"

As Tanya pulled away from the car park a blue and white slipped in behind her and flashed its headlights, she raised her hand to wave into the mirror.

"I reckon so, and sniff glue and shoot up and snort stuff. It's a constant worry when you have kids. We reckon we were really lucky our two haven't done any of that nonsense–" Kate stopped "–I suppose I should add, 'as far as we know.' I've programmed the location into the sat nav."

"Can you have a look on Google Earth and see where we can park. I don't want to get too close until we have a better idea what we're dealing with," Tanya said.

Kate scrolled and clicked on her tablet. "Okay, so there are six units. Four of them have boards showing their names. A tile warehouse, a battery supplier, car respray place, and something just called Big Dave's Cut Price. Hmm. The other two look as though they are possibly empty. Mind you, this image is over a year old. Anyway, we can park on a piece of spare ground in the middle of the estate."

"Have you got the co-ordinates for where the phone was picked up?"

"I have. It was a smart phone with GPS, and he had apps on there with location tracking as part of them. God bless kids and their apps. Anyway, it's up at the top end. There is one unit up there; it looks empty from the images but as I say they are not very current."

The rain was holding off for the moment but underfoot the ground was soft and puddly. Tanya wondered about fishing her boots out of the car, but it wasn't far to the tarmacked road and Kate was already some way ahead.

The unit was unlit and empty looking. Kate rattled the padlock holding a chain around the big gates and turned to raise her eyebrows. "Can we?" she asked.

"We have reason to believe there may be a young man in there and he may be in danger. Yes, I think we can. Hold on, I've got some tools in the boot." By the time she had taken the toolbox from her car the two uniformed officers had joined her.

"What do you need?"

"Something to deal with a padlock and chain."

"We've got bolt cutters. Dave'll go and get them for you?"

"Brilliant, thanks."

The heavy cutters made short work of the chain and they stomped across the empty car park to peer through the dirty windows. They could see nothing. The place was dark and deserted.

"Okay, we need to go in. The word is his phone was here somewhere. If it was, he's in trouble." Tanya turned to the bigger of the two men. "Do you think you can force the door?"

He pushed and rattled and kicked but came away shaking his head. "It's not going to be easy. It's metal and substantial. I don't know that even the Big Red Key would do it. We don't have one anyway. We could put in a call for a unit with the ram."

"Okay, let's see what the options are. I don't want to have to wait around if we can do this now. It's going to be dark soon." As she spoke Tanya set off down the side of the building. "I reckon we can justify breaking a window if we need to. Shit, there's rubble and stuff all down here." Now she wished she'd taken the time for the wellies. Her trouser hems were already muddy and wet, and the insides of her shoes were squelching with gritty water. "Kate, can you come in the top end of here? I'll meet you halfway."

"Coming down, boss."

Before Kate had struggled very far through the overgrown path, stepping over discarded paint cans and pieces of planking, they heard the shatter of breaking glass. The taller of the two uniformed guys appeared at the end of the building. Greg had found a little window with no bars, just a metal grill that came away from the wall.

"Alright, lads, just let's get on with it, shall we?"

It was a tight squeeze and undignified as she squirmed and kicked and pushed but, in the end, she did manage to finagle her way through the small gap.

It was a large vacant space apart from two small wooden chairs pulled together in the middle of the room. The door was locked solid and she could see no way to pick the lock. "I don't think there's anything here. There's another door in the corner, possibly a cupboard. I'll check in there, but I reckon this has been a waste of time. Maybe his phone was in a car or something. Hang on because I'll have to come back out through the window. I might need a hand."

The door opened easily. Tanya shone her torch around the storeroom, metal shelves, a couple of empty water bottles and in the corner the gleam of a patch of something drew her attention. A small pool of vomit, dry now and covered in ants.

Chapter 36

Tanya stood in the dark car park and tried to brush dirt from her trousers. "Nothing here, guys. You might as well get back to Snow Hill."

"Kate, get in touch with the technical department. See if they have an update on that bloody phone. If it was here, it's not now. I looked everywhere, there's nothing but a couple of chairs and a pool of puke."

"Thanks, lads. Sorry if it seems like a waste of time," Tanya said.

"It's okay, ma'am. Hope you find the kids."

Tanya's phone rang as they climbed back into the car. It was Brian Finch. "Tanya, are you coming back to Oxford tonight?"

"Yes, we're heading out now. No point in staying here in the dark."

"Great. Listen, come into headquarters, will you? I really need a word. I did ask the team to let you know."

"Yes, I'm aware. I've been a bit busy."

"Yeah, of course. Look, I really think it's important."

"Can't you tell me now? Kate's driving, we can talk."

"No, I'd prefer to discuss it face to face. If you can't make it, I'll go directly to Bob with this."

Tanya rolled her eyes and grimaced at Kate.

"I think you'd like to know about it," Brian said.

"I'll be back in a couple of hours. I'll see you then." She threw her phone onto the dashboard. "He can't help himself. He always has to let you know he's got friends in high places. Anyway, DI Finch has got some sort of bee in his bonnet. We'll swap at the next services and then I'll drop you off at home and go and find out what's eating him. You look done in. Oh yes, and be warned the bruising is quite colourful right now, hints of yellow here and there. Can't say it's an improvement. I'd avoid the mirrors if I were you."

"Thanks, boss." Kate touched her face with a fingertip. "To be honest, when you get to my age you tend to do that anyway. Look, if you're sure, I could do with a hot shower and bed. I'll be fine tomorrow. Do you want all the team in?"

Tanya blew out her cheeks. For a while she sat deep in thought. "No, I'll tell you what: if we don't get anything more on the phone trace, there's no real point. Thing is though, where do we go from here? Perhaps it would do everyone good to have a day off. I'll get in touch with some of my old contacts in missing persons and get them on board searching for these boys, and the girl, I think. I'll nag at the computer people in Birmingham. I had hoped we'd have had something from them about Jayden's activities by now. Not that we gave them much to go on. I hate this, I feel useless. Anyway, all in early on Monday. I'll arrange for any CCTV coverage in the area of the industrial park to be forwarded on. If the boy was there, then we might pick him up when he left. I'll ring his mum later, just to make sure he hasn't turned up at home. I think I'll see if we can get a CSI team into the warehouse place. If Birmingham can spare one. Someone had been there and not long ago. In fact, let me get on to it now." She made the call, lay back and closed her eyes. "It's a tangle, Kate. I just can't see my way through it yet, I can't find the connections and I'm bloody sure they are there."

"Your instincts have been spot on in the past, boss. Maybe you need a break as well. You've been at it non-stop since the first call came in. Then there is the stuff with Sue Rollinson."

"Yes. I wonder what Brian's found. He's spending a lot of time on it. Huh, could just be keeping his head down I suppose. Trying to look busy. By the way, do we know when the funeral is going to be?"

"Still waiting on word. Depending on the findings of the Health and Safety bods there may have to be an inquest. I hope they don't ask for a post-mortem. She died in hospital, under medical care so surely not."

"No, no. God, I hope not. It'll be a relief when we can put all this to bed at least."

* * *

The office was quiet, corridors dark. Tanya took a moment to glance into the incident room. There was evidence of the work that had been going on while she was away. Near the window she could see the pale glow of the whiteboard. She could see far too much white. They had so little to go on. She would update it in the morning, try to give the team some encouragement but it would be mostly window dressing. She closed the door and turned to her own office. The lights were low, but Brian Finch's computer lit the area around his desk with blue-white glow. He spun his chair round when he heard her come in.

"Brilliant. You made it."

"Yes, sorry it's so late but the traffic on the M40 was bloody awful."

"Nothing new there then. Right. I've been viewing the footage again. With what you noticed, just to cover all the bases. To be thorough." He paused and waited until she had acknowledged his statement.

It stuck in her craw, but she didn't have time to play his games.

"Well, I brought up all the other stuff we had from the area. Some of it was directly to do with Sue and what happened to her. But we had a fair bit more because you've been looking for those boys."

"Yes. I asked for everything available."

"Right, so we have some from the neighbour at the side of the house being renovated. It was the day before Sue's accident. The footage isn't very good, it's a cheap set-up, just black and white and pretty grainy so I printed off some stills. I was checking the scaffolding, how much they'd got done and what have you. Not much of it erected up until then but – there!" He pointed with his pen. "We can't see more than just the legs and the shadow because of the camera angle. It's male obviously, but difficult to say more than that."

"Okay."

"Well, what do you think he's doing?"

"I don't know. Building stuff," Tanya said.

"They've been laying concrete there. You can tell by the way the wood is laid around the edges and anyway the mixer is at the side – do you see, the frame and part of the drum?"

"Get to the point, Brian. I'm tired and grubby and I've still got to update my book."

He glared at her for a moment. She saw real anger in his eyes. "I could have gone straight to Bob with this. We need him to organise some work, but I wanted to give you the chance to have some input."

"Okay. Well, give me a clue. What am I looking for?"

"What do you know about laying concrete?"

"Bloody hell. Nothing, I'm not a builder. I know nothing about bricks and cement and, I don't know about, what do you call it, mortar?"

"Okay, well I've done some. We built a patio at the family house and one of the things you don't do is to mess about with it while it's drying."

"Okay. So, he's maybe fixing it somehow." She leaned in closer. "But I still don't understand. Sorry, Brian, you are going to have to spell this out for me."

He turned over another picture. "Look, the concrete there is damaged. All the path is smoothed except for one patch."

"Yes, I see. So, what are you telling me?"

"I reckon he's pushed something into the concrete."

"Let me see the footage," Tanya said.

"There's no need. I've got these images for the board. And there's this." He showed her yet another image. It was obviously taken earlier. "There, see there, he's got something in his hand. You can just make it out."

"Oh!"

"Yes, exactly. I wonder if we've found your weapon."

"Is there nothing on any of the other videos? I need to view them."

"No, not that I've seen, and we can't see where he went afterwards because he goes out of view after just a few paces. I've logged off now and honestly, these are the important bits. The rest of it is just concrete drying."

"What are your thoughts? About the image: young, old, what?"

"I would say not old. Jeans and trainers, he moves easily."

"Can this be Carl, or his mate? Young lads?"

Brian collected the prints together. He leaned back in his chair and grinned. "Could be."

"Well, first thing I guess is to get this enhanced." Tanya glanced at her watch. "No point even trying to contact anyone now. Soon as possible though."

"In the meantime, I'll have a word with Bob, tell him I've made a breakthrough," Brian said.

There were so many responses chasing each other through her mind. Tanya clenched her fists and took a deep breath. It didn't matter at this point, did it? Any forward movement was precious and if he needed the brownie points so be it. "Knock yourself out. I assume you'll be in tomorrow to follow this up."

"Tomorrow. Sunday."

"Well, yes. Not a problem, is it."

"No, of course – it's fine. See you in the morning."

As she collected her things together, she heard him on his mobile in the corridor. First to the DCI where he left a message and then to someone called Sophie. Apparently, the pub lunch was off.

Tanya smiled to herself as she walked to the car park.

Chapter 37

Carl had often imagined this. Riding in one of the big cars with Gregor. When he'd thought about it, he'd been sitting up front. Not driving yet, obviously, but in time – why not. What was happening now wasn't what he'd envisaged. Stuck in the back with Kayleigh, her legs jumping with nerves, up and down, up, and down. When he put his hand on her knee, she slapped it away. He could hear her breathing, fast and shallow as if she'd been running. His sister was terrified. Gregor was in the passenger seat and Stefan was driving. Their broad shoulders and thick necks filled the space in front.

As they brought them out of the warehouse he had, for one moment, considered running. He could outrun the big blokes he was sure. Then he remembered Kayleigh.

"So," he said. He tried to sound cool, in control but his voice came out high-pitched. The way it had been when it had been breaking last year, always at the wrong time, always when there was someone there to laugh at him. He coughed. "Where are we going? Are we going to pick up Jay?"

Gregor sighed. "Again with Jay. I've told you Jay is gone. You don't need to think about him. Better you think about you. Think about how you're going to pay me back. You owe me, boy."

"No, that's not right, Gregor. Honestly, I haven't got your money. I told you. It wasn't there. The money or the drugs. I looked in the cupboard, I looked everywhere. The police might have them, maybe one of the customers has double crossed you. Maybe the stupid old woman has done something with them. She kept saying she would."

He thought back to the times when she wasn't confused and upset by them arriving in the dark and pushing her around, taking food from her fridge and drinking her wine. On those days she had tried to persuade them to stop what they were doing. She had come up with plans. Stupid plans involving the police and then once an idea that if she threw the drugs away then the customers would stop coming. She didn't understand how it all worked. She didn't know who she was dealing with.

"Hey, Gregor. Maybe the old woman took the money. She was always moaning, always whining about how you'd lied to her when you pretended to want a tutor for your kid. She once said that she'd ring the police. She wanted to go to Australia, and she couldn't afford it. We stopped her, me and Jayden. We stopped her and made her see it was a bad idea to cross you. But, you know, maybe it was her."

The big man turned in his seat. "Maybe it was you. Maybe it was you and your skinny friend who took it and then you think – ah, Gregor he is stupid. We will kill this old woman, what use is she to anyone? We will kill her, and we will take the money and blame her. She can't talk, she is dead."

"No, no we didn't. I swear we didn't. She was already dead, well, dying anyway. We found her in the garden, and we ran. We couldn't go in the house, could we? Whoever killed her might have still been there."

Kayleigh had covered her mouth with her hands, her eyes were round and shocked. "What old woman, Carl. Not Granny. You're not talking about Granny." Carl reached across and squeezed her leg. He shook his head, but it was too late.

"No – not Granny. Another old woman. Something else, Kay. Nothing to do with you."

"You love your granny, eh?" Gregor said. The driver sniggered. "You like old ladies until you kill them. Maybe I go and see your granny. Maybe I'll tell her how much you like old ladies."

"Gregor, please." Carl felt tears pricking his eyes, but he wouldn't cry, not here, not in front of Stefan and his sister; he couldn't afford for either of them to think he was weak. He clenched his jaw and bit back the panic.

He glanced out of the window so they wouldn't see the glint of moisture in his eyes. He recognised where they were, but he didn't believe it. He tried to hold down the swell of hope but didn't have the control. "Are you taking us home?"

"You. I'm taking you home."

So, all the fear had been for nothing. He'd convinced them and it was all going to be okay. The big car pulled into the kerb a few yards away from their own house. Carl grabbed the handle and pulled but it was locked, of course it was. That was okay, it was to be expected. Kayleigh slid towards him, readying herself to clamber out.

Stefan turned off the engine and folded his arms across the steering wheel. Gregor climbed out and passed in front of the car and round to the back door.

As the door opened, Carl swung round to jump out. Gregor grabbed the edge of the door and slammed it back hard onto Carl's legs where they dangled unsupported between the car and the road. His scream was high and hard, Kayleigh behind him screeched more with shock than knowledge of what had happened.

This time there was no way he could hold back the tears of pain. Gregor pulled the door away and Carl bent forward grabbing at his legs, rubbing to ease the agony. He was sobbing and staring down to where his jeans were

157

discolouring with dark stains. He felt the warm trickle of blood on his shins.

As he leaned to pull up his trousers to see the damage, Gregor grabbed his face in one of his big hands. He squeezed hard, a thumb on one cheek, his thick powerful fingers on the other, and he forced Carl to look at him. "Now, you go into your house, boy. You tell no-one. You owe me big. You wait and I will send someone. They will bring some product and an address and instructions. You will not lose my money this time, boy. You will do as you are told and you will not mention this to anyone, not to the police, not to your whore of a mother, no-one." With the final threat, he dragged Carl from the car and let him fall to the pavement, squirming backwards, rubbing at his damaged legs.

Kayleigh had begun to climb down but Gregor pushed her back, a hand on her chest, the other gathering up her legs and twisting them back inside. "No, you stay here."

He turned and put a foot on Carl's ankle, just enough pressure to force him to stillness. Carl reached up with one hand. "No, Gregor, please. Let her out. Just let her out. I'll do whatever you want. Just let her come out. She hasn't done anything. She didn't know anything."

"She will come with us. If she comes back…" He shrugged. "That is up to you, boy. You do as I ask until you have paid me back and maybe she can come home. If not…" He kicked Carl's legs out of his way, walked back around the front of the car, climbed in, and slammed the door.

As the big black vehicle drove away, Carl could see Kayleigh's pale face in the rear window, her fists thumping on the glass. He watched until they turned the corner and then staggered to his feet. Whimpering, he dragged himself the few yards to his front gate and up the narrow path to his front door.

Chapter 38

Tanya was grubby and felt dead on her feet but even after a hot shower, a slice of defrosted chicken pie and two glasses of wine, she couldn't settle. She updated her book and over and over was drawn back to the video footage. She paused it, replayed it, zoomed in and out but the quality was poor, and the angles were all wrong. She agreed Finch was probably right. The object visible for a short couple of frames looked like a knife. She made a note to have Simon Hewitt have a look – the medical examiner could tell whether it was at least the right sort of length and shape. There was only one way to find out and first thing in the morning she would set things in motion. The newly laid path was going to be dug up.

The knife had been buried for almost a week. Wet, dirty, and covered in cement – the chance of prints and DNA would have to be zero. Even if they could have Carol Barker's daughter identify it as one from the house, and what a cruel thing to do to a woman who was already medically compromised, it wouldn't help very much.

They had to find more film of the bloke. The jeans would be no help, on this footage they were just a dark grey shape, no label, no fancy stitching. The trainers might be the best bet. If they could identify the make and then find the same type in Carl's or Jayden's bedroom, it would be something. They could bring them in, look for soil in the sole, cement in the uppers, blood in the inners. To do it though, they needed to have them in the lab. Jayden's mum would probably be helpful but taking anything from Carl's house would most likely present a problem. They needed convincing evidence that the grey, wavering figure was one of the boys.

She was so tired the lines of text began to blur but she was still buzzing, events playing over and over. No point going to bed, not yet. It was after ten, was it too late to call Charlie? She'd send him a message, that wouldn't wake Joshua and Carol. Moments after she pressed send, her phone rang. With a smile she read Charlie's name on her screen.

"Hiya, Charlie. I hope I didn't disturb you."

"No, it's fine. Actually, Joshua isn't well so I'm sitting here on the couch with him snuggled up in a blanket. Giving Carol the chance to have some sleep."

"Oh blimey, sorry. I don't want to disturb him. What's wrong?"

"Oh, poor little bugger's got croup. It's okay though, he's had some Calpol. He's spark out for the moment but I've got a thing making steam on the coffee table."

Tanya hadn't a clue what croup might be and the reason you would want to make steam flummoxed her completely, and what the heck was Calpol? She made some sympathetic noises and it seemed enough.

"How are things going with your murder?" Charlie asked.

"Not good. Slow and difficult. Listen though, can I ask you a question? You don't have to answer if you don't want to."

"Fire away."

"A while ago, when he first joined us, you told me you had heard some stuff about Finch when you were at Hendon."

"Yes. I thought he'd moved on from you – gone to Sheffield or somewhere."

"Birmingham. But we've got him back. I heard some talk about him today though and I wondered if it was similar to what you knew from back then, from the college. Apparently, he can be a bit of a bully, does it sound likely to you?"

There was a long silence and she could hear Charlie breathing at the other end. "I never saw anything myself so I don't like to comment really but let me just say I wouldn't discount it. Has he upset you, Tanya?"

"God, no. It'd take more than him. But I'm thinking of the team. We are working with him again just now and if there is anything I need to watch for, it's better I know about it."

"Ha, is this the DI Miller I've come to know?"

"What, what do you mean?"

"Sorry, maybe that was out of line."

"No, no come on, Charlie, tell me what you mean."

"Well, you know – you didn't use to be so concerned with the feelings of colleagues, did you? I mean you've really become much more of a team player lately. You've always been a great detective, you know I think that, but this, this caring is good, it's great."

She heard the wail of the sick baby. It was sad and disturbing. "Oh, look you've got to go. I'll talk to you soon. I hope he gets better really quickly."

She sat back in the living room, turning the small handset between her fingers. It was true, she did care more than she used to. She'd come to know the people she worked with, their strengths and their failings. Then she had a vision of the limp and broken body of Sue Rollinson as they dug her out from under the scaffolding. That was her fault, wasn't it? If she really cared, she wouldn't have sent the young woman off on her own just because she was impatient. Brian Finch was supposed to be looking into the incident and now he'd headed off at a tangent and was excited and wrapped up in her own case. What did this mean for Sue and her accident? She groaned and poured herself another glass of wine.

Chapter 39

Carl knew there was a first aid kit somewhere. It used to be in the kitchen cupboard when they'd all been together, when things were good. There were bandages, and sticking plasters, and Savlon. A white box it was, with a red cross on the front. Dragging empty bottles and dirty rags out of the cupboard under the sink he threw them behind him, his jeans stuck to the front of his legs, where the blood dried and pulled at the wounds when he moved. Kneeling on the tiles the pain was horrible.

He found it, dirty and dented at the back, and dragged it out. He could hear himself groaning, tried to stop it, moved, and groaned again. His hands shook and it took him three tries to flip up the little metal catch. The bandages were in discoloured paper wrappings, and the plasters no longer sticky enough to be any good. The tube of cream was well out of date, squeezed out of shape in the middle and crusty around the top.

He tried first to pull up his trouser legs, hissing with the pain of it. Then he lay on the floor and wriggled them down. "Shit." Bruises, blackened already, split skin, trickles of blood and red staining down his shins. If the door had hit his knees he would have been crippled. But it hadn't and he wasn't, so all he needed to do was man up and get this sorted. His sister was more important than battered legs and he had to do something.

He was squeezing cream on an open wound he thought probably needed some stitches. He knew these days they glued cuts together, but did they use ordinary Super Glue – didn't matter really, they probably hadn't got any anyway. He laid a piece of lint over the worst bits and wrapped an elastic bandage around it to hold it in place. Then he did the same on the other leg tucking the ends in. He gathered up his stained jeans and threw them into the machine. Pulling at his sweatshirt he shrugged, probably an idea to stick that in as well, it was pretty rank and anyway there might be evidence on it. He held the top in front of him. Evidence of what? In the great play of things what had really been done here?

Okay, the drugs – illegal. Scaring the old woman – unkind. But he hadn't started all that. There was some shoplifting, riding without buying tickets – well, that was just what he did, what was so wrong with that? They hadn't broken into the woman's house. They always used the key – yes, they nicked her food and her booze and Jayden had taken some money from her purse and a couple of gold chains she'd left lying about. It was nothing – it was kids' stuff. It was small change. If he had to answer for all those things, how bad could it be? A bit of community service – a stretch at a young offender's place. He could do it, no problem, of course he could. It wasn't him who had picked her out and tricked her into holding the money in the first place and then told her she'd broken the law so she couldn't back out. That had been Gregor's work. The thoughts unwound themselves as he limped up the stairs and stripped off the rest of his clothes in the bathroom.

He wanted a shower but that would mess up the dressings on his legs. He leaned over the bath and turned on the water to let it spray down on his head and upper body. It warmed him; his muscles began to soften. Rubbing at his hair with his own thick, fluffy towel, the one he kept in his own room, hidden from his mother, he let the musings run on to the end. He was out of his depth. He didn't know where his mate was, but he did know his sister was in the brutal hands of Gregor and his thugs. There was no way he could deal with this on his own. He heard his mother. She came out of her bedroom and crossed the landing, she thumped into the wall on the way to the toilet. Stoned or drunk or maybe both. No help there.

His phone rang. Unknown number. Jay! Or Gregor. He clicked the answer button and held it to his ear in silence.

"Carl, is that you? It's me, Lydie. Carl, where's my Jay? Do you know? I haven't seen him in days, the police have been here. I can't get him on the phone. What have you been doing? What bad stuff have you got into? Tell me, Carl. Please. I'll help you. I'll help you both. We can go to the police together. Please, Carl, I just want my boy home." Then she started to cry.

He didn't know what to say, what to do, so he cut the call, turned his phone to silent and put it under his pillow.

There had been something on the radio about the dead woman. He couldn't remember where he heard it. He pulled out his phone again. Googled the BBC news, scrolled and clicked and eventually he found it on the local radio station for Oxford. A number to call. What would happen then? Would they arrest him? Would they protect him from Gregor – could they? Would they just bloody go and find Kayleigh, if he made them see she was the only thing that mattered, he had come to them because of her. Were they good enough to do that? They screwed up a lot – look at the times they'd let a terrorist slip through their fingers. They were pillocks most of them. Would they have a clue how to find her, how to bring her home?

He googled the detective. She was just a woman. Not bad looking, pretty fit really but she was old, at least thirty-five and looked a bit like a teacher. No make-up, a serious face. But she was one of them, the feds – babylon. Would she listen, understand what he was telling her? Would she just see him as the answer to her problem, solving the murder and ignoring the scatter of other harm and danger? Perhaps she would write his sister off as collateral damage. He had no misconceptions; he knew his family were about the lowest of the low in society.

Who could he trust?

Chapter 40

The chirp of her phone dragged Tanya back from deep sleep and she pawed at the bedside table with her eyes still closed to find the device. "Miller." Her voice was sluggish and thick. She pushed herself into a sitting position and rubbed at her eyes.

"Sorry, boss. It's Dan."

"Yeah, it's okay, Dan."

"I'm sorry to wake you, but I thought you'd want the news."

"It's fine, really. What have you got for me?"

"I was in early and have been going through the CCTV footage from Birmingham. I've picked up a black Range Rover, going towards the industrial estate. A few times in the last few weeks and more often in the last days. I think it might be worth having the technical department enhancing the images to see just who is inside. But it looks to me as though it went in the last time, Saturday, with one driver and passenger and there were two more passengers in the rear when it left. More than that though, I've tracked it to Carl Grant's house. Not all the way there but near enough for it to be a possible destination. Unfortunately, there is no cover in the street itself."

"I'm coming in, Dan. Just give me half an hour. Excellent work. How come you were in so early? How come you were in at all? Oh, never mind, doesn't matter. I'll be going up to Birmingham. Oh bugger, there's something else. We think we have found the weapon."

"Great!"

"Well yes, it is but I need to organise for it to be dug out of a slab of concrete. Someone will have to speak to DCI Scunthorpe to authorise it. We'll need equipment. It'll have to be Brian Finch. Okay – sorry, Dan – I'm rambling. Look, put the coffee on. I'll be with you shortly and you'll be coming to Birmingham. Is there any news about a CSI team going to the warehouse?"

"I haven't seen anything."

* * *

By the time she arrived at the office Dan had printed out stills of the car and stuck them on the whiteboard. He had contacted the technical bods and forwarded the footage on to them and he had slipped out to buy pastries to go with their coffee. Tanya could have hugged him. She had to make do with another '*Excellent work, Dan. Thanks.*'

There was no way around it. Finch was going to have to be left in charge. If Carl Grant was back at his house she needed to be there too. She toyed briefly with the idea of asking Kate to come in to keep an eye on the DI, to report back. But it was wrong, Lewis needed a day off and she couldn't put her in such a position.

She had the phone on speaker, typing one-handed to send an email to Snow Hill, hurrying them along with the examination of the unit, and with the other hand she stuffed a croissant into her mouth. It was undignified but she had realised on the way in that, apart from a small piece of pie, she had eaten next to nothing over the last few days. The pastry was sweet, buttery, and delicious and she dragged the box towards her to pick out another one. Of course, he answered just as she had taken a mouthful.

"Brian, there's been a development and I need to go to Birmingham. I'm taking DC Price with me. Can you bring DCI Scunthorpe up to date and get things started with the weapon search? It's going to be complicated."

"Of course. No problem. I'll ring Bob on the way in."

"Brian. While you're here, how is it going regarding Sue's accident? Are you any closer to a decision? It'd be good to be able to let her family know they can start to organise the funeral, wouldn't it? They can't move on and it must be torture for them."

"I'm doing a thorough job with that. I feel, as it's a colleague it's the least she deserves," Brian said.

"Yes, of course, absolutely, I understand that. I just wondered is all."

"It'll take as long as it takes, Tanya. I'm looking at footage from around the area."

"But why?"

"Because I think it's necessary. When I've reached a conclusion, I'll let you know. I am fully aware this is time-sensitive, but I need to know I did the best job I could."

"From what I understand the Health and Safety Executive working with the builders have reached their conclusions and deemed it an accident because the scaffolding was under construction. The company will be censured because Sue was able to gain access to the site without supervision but there were warning signs she ignored. Have you seen their report?"

"Of course, I have. It was interesting and when I'm ready I'll share my findings."

"Well if another head would help, you know where I am. Did you follow up my idea that she was speaking to someone?"

"Thanks, Tanya, but I've got this."

She had no more time to argue. Dan was waiting at the office door and with a curt "Goodbye," she flung the handset back into its cradle.

Chapter 41

They didn't take Tanya's car but opted instead to take one of the pool vehicles, one with a bit more oomph. Dan was pleased when she asked him to drive. "You contacted Snow Hill, didn't you? Asked for someone to watch the house?" Tanya said.

"I did. I thought I told you."

"Yes, I think you did. It was early and I wasn't firing on all cylinders. Just double checking. We'll go straight to the house but park at the far end of the road. If we can get there without him realising it'll save us a lot of grief. If he's still there, of course."

"You're not going to ring his mum then?"

"God, no. The woman's a liability, we've no idea how she might react. No, let's just try and take him by surprise."

"If he's just a youngster won't you need a responsible adult? You know, in case his mum's not there, or drunk, or whatever."

"Not now. I'm only going to interview him as a witness, well not really even that and he is fourteen. All we know is he was in the vicinity of the house on the day Carol Barker was killed and we believe it was him who clobbered DC Lewis. If things change and they very well might, then I'll make the call."

They drove in silence for a while. The roads weren't too busy, it was still early. Tanya looked over at the young detective. "So, how are you doing with the preparations for your promotion exam? I'm sorry, Dan, I haven't been around much. But you know, if I can help just let me know. I'll make time."

He glanced across the car and grinned at her. He was lovely-looking. His dark blond hair had been left to grow longer and curled a bit on the back of his neck. She knew he worked out and it showed in the bulge of the muscles of his arms as he turned the wheel taking them into the overtaking lane. She felt safe in the car with him, though he drove fast she didn't experience the clench of nerves in her stomach the way she did with Brian Finch the couple of times she had ridden with him. There was no antagonism, just skill. Dan didn't seem out to prove anything and yet she knew he was shy, diffident. His confidence had grown since she had known him and now he was calm, in control and restful to be with. She had the fleeting thought that it was a shame he batted for the other team and then pushed it away as wrong. But it reminded her, no matter how far society had progressed it would be a long time before all the old prejudices were dead even with people who didn't hold to them. That brought other thoughts to the fore. "So, is Brian Finch back with us?"

"Yes. That was a bit of a surprise. I thought he'd gone for good. Impressing them up in Birmingham, moving on, moving up."

"Hmm. You get on okay, do you?"

He made a noncommittal shrug.

"You've worked with him quite closely on a couple of things?" She was pushing it but there was a part of her that wanted something, something to disapprove of when she dealt with the other DI.

"Now and then," Dan said.

It was going nowhere, and she had to let it drop as they neared the turnoff for Birmingham, and she set the sat nav to take them to Carl's house.

Sunday, mid-morning. Not much going on really. They passed a retail park buzzing with life, a church with three cars parked outside. In the street where Carl lived there were a couple of joggers and one resident cleaning his car at the roadside.

After a quick word with the two officers in the patrol car, Tanya and Dan walked down to hammer on the door at the scruffy little house. After a short wait they knocked again. Dan stepped back, peered up at the upstairs windows.

After a couple more minutes they heard the rattle of the security chain and Mrs Grant looked out at them through the narrow gap. "Oh right, you again."

"Can we come in, Mrs Grant?" Tanya said.

"No."

"We need to have a word with your son. He is here, isn't he?"

"No."

"I'm sorry. I don't believe you. We have information that tells us he is here, and we really need to see him. What about your daughter, is she here?"

"I don't bloody know, do I? She might be. I've not been well. Been in bed. You should leave people alone."

"Mrs Grant, let us in. We don't want to have to get a warrant." With a sigh the woman stepped back, as Tanya had known she would, and gave them access.

As they walked into the stale-smelling hallway, they heard the clatter from the kitchen. Dan Price pushed past and raced through the narrow space. Fighting with furniture, empty bottles and bags discarded on the floor he struggled through and dragged opened the back door. "He's legged it, boss, over the back fence."

He ran across the neglected garden and pulled himself up on the rickety wooden fence. As he braced his arms and threw his leg upward, the old, dried out wood cracked and complained. Under the strain of the assault it leaned and tilted and tipped backwards depositing the detective in the overgrown, weedy grass at the bottom of the garden.

Tanya had spun on her heels and left the house by way of the front door. Two houses further along the street there was a narrow passage allowing access to the backs of the properties and a footpath behind the rear gardens. She gave a frantic wave to the parked patrol car, but they had obviously switched into lower gear knowing she was in the house. She would see they answered for that later. She shot down the alleyway and spotted the slight figure of Carl Grant pounding away from her, heading in the direction of the main road.

There was no point in shouting. *Stop, Police!* would carry no sway with the fleeing boy, so she saved her breath for the chase.

He was fast, she was fast, but he had the edge and she knew she would lose him. If it hadn't been for the cat, she would have lost him. It came from nowhere, curling out from an open gateway. It was part way out before it registered the boy. It stopped and rounded on him, back arched, head down, ears flattened. He didn't see it. He didn't mean to kick it, but the speed and the panic carried him forward to trip, head over heels his arms flying out to break his fall. The cat screeched and ran, leaving Carl sprawled on the flagstones.

It gave Tanya the chance she needed to catch him. By the time he had gathered himself, rolled and scrambled to his feet she had gained precious yards. "Carl!" Now there might be a point to shouting. "Wait. I need to talk to you."

She ran on. He bent and fumbled at the edge of the wall and then straightened and turned towards her. She was almost upon him. She nearly had him. Then she saw the knife, a six-inch serrated blade, a vicious point, and his face, frightened and angry and out of control. He crouched, poised to strike.

"Come on then, bitch. You want some of this? Come on then."

Chapter 42

Tanya had been here before. She had faced a knife when she'd been searching for her kidnapped niece. That time had ended with a horrible injury to her arm. It had taken weeks to heal properly and she was still not convinced it was as strong as it should be. Her heart pounded, fear came in and turned her stomach. She felt the ghost of the wound.

She took a step forward, reached out towards the frantic boy. "Carl, come on now. You don't need to do this. We only need to talk to you. Just put the knife down and we'll go back home and have a chat."

He was spooked, looking for a way out. Seeking salvation. Tanya took another small step.

"No, no you stay there. I'll cut you. Don't think I won't."

"Carl. Calm down. There's no need for this. It's just making things worse. All we want to do is to talk to you."

He was walking backwards, slowly, sliding his feet on the gritty ground. Every so often he would glance behind, but the knife was held in front, jagging and jerking. She could take him down, there was no doubt, but not if the blade got her first. The alleyway was narrow, lined on both sides by garden walls. There were gates at regular intervals, most were closed but now and then one hung open.

She could see the fear in his eyes, his hand was unsteady holding the weapon. On the edge of total meltdown, terrified. She could use that. She could wind up the tension, scare him even more. But if she did it could go either way. It was possible he would give it up and let her take him or – it was a strong possibility – he could lose what little control he still had and hurt her, or himself or them both. At this point there was no way to tell, it was down to luck far more than good judgement.

"It doesn't make any difference what you do to me, Carl. You can stick me with that thing" – Tanya raised a hand and pointed – "the place is full of police. My mate will have radioed it in by now. They'll be everywhere. Have you any idea what they'll do to you if you hurt me, if you stab one of their own? Oh yes, there are rules but not when one of our colleagues is involved, not then. All rules go by the board. They'll take you down. You won't know what's hit you." She heard a siren in the distance.

"Do you hear that, Carl? Can you hear them coming? You don't stand a chance. Not a chance. You might as well give it up now. Just hand over the weapon and come with me. All I want to do is talk to you. I don't know whether you've done anything wrong – but don't you see? – all this, it just makes you look guilty. You've already committed an offence by running away." It wasn't true but she didn't think he'd know that. "You're just digging yourself further and further in."

Dan turned in at the end of the alleyway, quiet and slow. She resisted the temptation to raise her gaze. She could see him in her peripheral vision, just over Carl's shoulder, she mustn't look. She stared straight at the boy, fixed her eyes on his face. "Come on, just come with me."

She moved again, half a step. "Stop it." As he spoke Carl gave a small leap forward, knees bent, leaning with his arm stretched, shoulders hunched.

Dan was creeping onward, close against the wall, steady and careful. Focused. She mustn't look up. Not know, not when he was nearly there.

"I've told you, bitch. Stand still. Leave me alone. I'm not talking to you, not talking to anyone. You don't know what this is about. You don't know. Leave me alone. I haven't done anything." He had stopped now, straightened, looking her in the eye.

"Okay, if you haven't done anything just come and talk to us. We're trying to find your friend. Jayden's mum is worried about him. She doesn't know where he is. Do you?"

"No. No, I don't know. I haven't seen him. Leave him out of this. This isn't about Jay."

"I think it is…"

Dan was just a few short steps away, almost upon them.

The bottle was hidden in the grass growing at the base of the wall. Dan was focused on the boy, on Tanya, edging forward, step by step. His foot hit the bottle, knocking it in front of him on to the flagstones, clattering and chinking rolling forward. Carl spun at the sound, saw the other man, lashed out with the knife missing Dan's belly by inches. The force of the thrust unbalanced him, he toppled, and Tanya ran to push him to the ground. She threw herself on top of him, knee in the middle of his back, grabbing at his arms, shaking, shaking the knife free so it fell with a clatter against the wall.

They didn't cuff him. He had pulled a weapon on a police officer, they had grounds to arrest him, but she wanted him to talk to them. Arresting him now would put him in the system, legal representatives, responsible adults, probably medical intervention to make sure he wasn't hurt. It would take forever, and they needed to talk to him now.

She dragged him to his feet and holding him between them they marched him back down the alley towards his house. He sniffed and sobbed and made no further attempt to escape.

Chapter 43

Carl curled up in a chair by the fireplace. He hadn't spoken since they marched him back into the house. His mother stood in front of the window puffing desperately at a cigarette. Now and then she would turn to look at her son, at the two officers on the settee, and shake her head. Her thin body was riven with tremors and her skinny arms wrapped around her as if for warmth. The house was stuffy and stale-smelling.

Tanya leaned forward. "Carl, we know there has been something really bad going on. If you've been involved, it will be better for you if you tell us about it now. But at least tell us, if you know, where Jayden is. His mum is going out of her mind. We'll get to the rest later."

Here Frances Grant spun to look into the room. "Never mind bloody Jayden. What about my Kayleigh. Hello! My daughter's missing. Nobody interested in that, are they? Oh no. What are you doing about that, Mrs Detective whatever your name is?"

Dan answered, "Of course we're concerned about Kayleigh, Mrs Grant. Of course we are. But we need Carl to tell us what he knows about all of this. We need to find them both and sort this out. Now, please why don't you sit down. I'll make us a cup of tea, shall I?"

"Coffee – strong and black. There's a jar in the cupboard." She sniffed and rubbed a hand under her nose. "Carl, stop buggering about and just tell them what they want to know. I have to be in work in an hour, I've got a shift cleaning at the pub. Just tell 'em and then they can sod off out of here."

"Mrs Grant, please can you just leave this up to us. Give your son a chance to talk." Tanya moved along the settee to the place Dan had vacated, nearer to the boy. He still had his head lowered almost to his knees, he picked and pulled at the fabric of his jeans and now and then kicked with his heel at the threadbare carpet.

"If you don't talk to us, Carl, we are going to have no choice but to take you down to the station. That's going to take time and involve a lot of other people," Tanya said.

"No!" He looked at her now, fear widening his eyes. "You can't. Mum, don't let them take me."

"I won't, son. Don't you worry, they're not taking you anywhere."

"I'm sorry, Mrs Grant, it's not going to be your choice to make. If I believe Carl has information that will help us with our enquiries, then I can take him in. We had hoped not to but unless he tells us what he knows…" Tanya shrugged.

"You can't. It'll make everything worse," Carl said. "Why can't you just leave me alone. If you leave me alone, I can sort this. Just give me time."

Tanya shook her head. "I'm sorry, Carl, just not happening."

"Look, he's not done anything. He hasn't taken Jayden away, he doesn't know where Kayleigh is, leave him be. I'll have you for this. This is harassment."

"Mrs Grant…" Tanya was losing patience with the woman. It was time to move things along. "Okay, Carl. We'll leave that part for the time being. I also must ask you whether you have been to Oxford in the last few days. Before you answer I need you to know we have video footage of a person answering your description in the vicinity of a house where a serious crime has been committed. So, be very careful how you answer. If you lie to us about this, it won't look good. If you don't answer I'm going to have no choice but to take you to the station and interview you under caution. It all gets much more serious then, Carl."

He was nibbling around his fingernails and as she finished speaking, he looked up at her, spit a small piece of skin and coughed. "We didn't do anything. Not that day."

His voice was low, gravelled by fear but Tanya wouldn't ask him to repeat it. He was speaking, she wouldn't interrupt. She leaned a little closer.

"We went down just like usual. We went across the spare ground and over the fence. Jayden was over first, and I heard him, he sort of gasped and then he started swearing. When I got over, I saw her. Under the tree. She was lying under the tree."

He started to shake now. It had all become too much for him. They should have him seen by a doctor, his mother could insist on it, but she was still peering through the window, lighting another cigarette. Tanya wasn't even sure she was listening anymore.

"What did you do?"

"We couldn't do nothing. We didn't know what to do. We just legged it."

"You left her there, bleeding on the grass?" Tanya struggled to keep the disbelief from her voice. "Why would you do that? Why didn't you at least call for help?"

She knew Dan stood in the doorway with the tray of cups, she also knew he wouldn't come in, not now – not when they had broken through.

"No. We just ran. We were scared, weren't we? We didn't know if they were still there. Whoever had stuck her. They could have been there, and they could have been waiting for us."

"Why would they have been waiting for you? I don't understand."

She watched as the reality dawned on him. As he acknowledged that he could never go back, Carl glanced around the room, panic flaring in his eyes again and then they saw him give it up. Acceptance and exhaustion drove out the last vestige of struggle and he flopped back in his chair and closed his eyes.

"We thought it might be one of Gregor's rivals. We thought it could be just some random punter. The old woman could never keep her mouth shut. She was always coming up with plans and ideas to get us out of it. She was always saying she wanted to help us. Stupid cow. Nobody could help us. We didn't want nobody to help us."

Frances Grant had turned to face the room. "Carl. Stop. Jesus, don't say anymore." Her son raised his head and looked at her. He gave a small smile.

"It's okay, Mum. It's for the best. It's time to stop it all. It's all gone bad and we need to get Kay home. It'll be okay."

She began to cry but he turned back to Tanya. "If I tell you, you have to promise you'll find Kayleigh. Gregor's got her. If he finds out I've talked to you…"

Frances Grant let out a high wail. Carl glanced at her.

"I'm sorry, Mum, I thought I'd make it work. I thought I'd fix things, but I couldn't, and I don't know what to do now." He turned back to Tanya. "I don't know but I think maybe Jay is dead."

He couldn't continue and as he dissolved into gulping sobs Tanya pulled out her phone to call for a car to come and take him to the station.

Chapter 44

There was no other choice but to take him to the police station and interview Carl under caution. As they followed the patrol car towards Snow Hill, Tanya made the call to arrange an interview room.

"How much do you believe, Dan?" Tanya asked.

"I have to say, I think what he has told us, precious little up to now of course, but I believe him. He's worried sick about his sister. That's got to be our priority, hasn't it? Finding her and getting her to safety."

"Absolutely, I just hope we're not too late. And Jayden, what do you reckon there? I really don't want to have to take bad news to Lydie Gormon. I've asked Kate to get on with the search on this Gregor. We need more detail. Where he came from, what he does, what property he owns. We need to know why he would kill Carol Barker if she was useful to him."

"Or what other gang might have been involved. I wouldn't have thought this would come down to a turf war. Every time I think I've seen it all something else comes up. They say money is the root of all evil, but it's not, is it? It's drugs," Dan said.

"Money is the cause of a lot of trouble though, isn't it?"

Tanya leaned back in the car seat, thoroughly exhausted and depressed.

* * *

Carl told them all he knew. He opened up about his mother's drug habit, not that it was any surprise. He admitted carrying drugs and money from Birmingham to Oxford and how they had bullied and terrorized the old woman once Gregor's thugs had set up the drop at her home. He pleaded with them to find his sister and his best friend, and told them the few places he thought Gregor might be found. Mostly, though, the handovers had been done on dark streets, in car parks, now and then in McDonald's. They had only used the industrial unit once while he'd been a courier. But when the CSI team handed in a preliminary report of drug residue in the building, he showed no surprise. However, when Tanya read out to him the information that blood had been found, and hair, he dissolved into tears and they could get no further with the questioning until he had been seen by a doctor.

Tanya and Dan sat in the canteen. He was devouring a bacon sandwich as if he'd never seen food before. Tanya played with the stirring stick in her cup of coffee. "We're going to have to arrest him, once the medic gives the all clear. I'll put it off as long as I can. Once we've done that, we'll be lucky to get any more information. A solicitor is going to keep him quiet. Let's go and see if they've managed to track the Range Rover. How hard can it be? There are bloody cameras everywhere."

"Yes, but Birmingham, the roads round here are manic, aren't they?"

"Busy yes, but we know what we're looking for. Have you nearly finished that?" She pointed at the bread roll.

Dan stuffed the last greasy bite into his mouth, wiped his fingers and dabbed at his lips. He pushed back from the table. As they turned away, a uniformed officer appeared in the doorway, scanning the room.

"Detective Inspector Miller?"

Tanya nodded.

"We've found the car. It's out near Solihull, one of the big houses. DCI Parker is waiting to speak to you."

"Brilliant. Thanks." They scurried through the building to find the DCI pacing back and forth in his office. "DI Miller, I've spoken with DCI Scunthorpe. I've agreed to let you lead this. We need to get that girl to safety, and it might be quicker as you're already up to speed. I understand there is a missing boy as well."

"Sir. Thank you. What manpower can you let me have?"

"Whatever you need. I've already asked them to mobilize a team, they'll be down in the car park by the time you get there."

"Thank you, sir."

The drive from the city to the suburbs was fast and noisy. Four vehicles, sirens blaring, tyres screeching on the bends. As they neared the affluent area – large houses, a park, a couple of schools – they drew into the side of the road for Tanya to confer with the armed response team commander.

He was experienced and there to take care of business and Tanya deferred to his expertise. "Just keep out of the way and I'll get you in there as soon as I can," he told her.

Though they lined the street with dark-clad, armed officers, though they had brought the battering ram, though they were wound up and ready for confrontation, everything was over quickly, calmly. The front door was opened by a young man dressed in jeans and a hoody. He glanced at the armed officers, raised his eyebrows, and then opened the door wide, stood back and ushered Tanya, the firearms officer and Dan inside with a sweep of his arm. It was faintly embarrassing.

A bulky man in dark trousers and a black sweater met them in the hallway of the gracious house. "Good afternoon, gentlemen, lady. I am Gregor. This is my home. How can I help you today?"

Chapter 45

They weren't surprised he insisted on reading the warrant to search his house. They weren't surprised when Gregor told them he was calling his lawyer. They were a little surprised when he ushered them into the bright living room and offered them coffee.

"I trust your people will take care while they search my home," he said.

He refused to answer much other than to confirm his name, Gregor Belic, that his age was forty-two and that he was originally from Serbia. When Tanya asked him his profession, he gave a short shake of his head. "I am a businessman. I have several concerns." The young man who had answered the door brought in a tray of drinks and biscuits. It was surreal. They had come expecting confrontation, maybe danger and instead they had tea and digestives. Tanya was overwhelmingly tired, and she was swept by the absurd need to laugh. She fought hard to hold down a giggle. Dan, sitting opposite to her tipped his head to one side, frowned. She pulled herself together, remembered the body under the tree, the woman in Australia now in hospital and her mood settled. She really needed to get some proper rest. But not now. Not until this was finished.

She took out pictures of Jayden and Carl. "Do you know these young men, Mr Belic?"

He glanced at the images. Pulled down the corners of his mouth and shrugged. "I don't think I shall answer any questions until my lawyer arrives."

"And this young woman?" She placed the picture of Kayleigh on the coffee table. She didn't want to tell him what Carl had said. Didn't want to put the boy in more danger than he already was. She was trying to avoid letting Gregor know they had the teenager. Even in custody he was still at risk, it was no good pretending otherwise. If this bloke was the kingpin of a drug gang his reach would be long, his influence in detention centres frightening. "We have CCTV of this young woman in a car which we believe belongs to you. We also have footage of her close to one of your properties, a storage unit. As I am sure you know the unit has been searched and we have found evidence of drugs and we have found blood there. What can you tell me about that?"

"I am waiting for my legal advisor. I know nothing about a storage unit. I have many properties; they are rented out. I am, as I said, a businessman."

They could hear the thump of boots in the upstairs rooms, doors opening and closing and then the clatter of people running back down the stairs. Through the long windows they watched as more officers stomped around the garden, poked under shrubs and bushes, and pulled bins and garden furniture about. They opened the shed and one of them disappeared inside, but it was clear they were finding nothing. As two of them removed the top of the compost bin and poked into it with sticks, Tanya sat straighter, glaring out. She didn't want them to find anything out there. If they did it would mean she had failed, she had let everyone down. With a sense of relief, she watched as they reclosed the composter and turned away.

She didn't drink the tea. They didn't eat the biscuits and when one of the black-clad figures appeared in the doorway to shake his head, Tanya simply nodded in response.

They heard the crunch of a car on the gravel outside. Shortly afterwards, Gregor's lawyer walked into the room. He placed his briefcase on the floor beside the table and held out his hand. "Warrant."

Dan handed it to him.

"I trust you have not been questioning my client." He turned now and shook Gregor's hand. "I'll have this sorted soon, Mr Belic. Don't worry."

It was as they had expected, 'No comment. No comment. No comment.' They were wasting time and eventually Tanya had to acknowledge they were going to get nowhere. The evidence they had from Carl wasn't strong enough to take this man in. The boy was scared, had admitted wrongdoing and once they went down the route of arrest and questioning, the clock would start ticking. They didn't have the time to waste, they had to find Kayleigh and Jay.

Tanya glanced at Dan, picked up her bag and stepped towards the door. Before she left the room, she turned. "I will see you again, Mr Belic. I truly think that. For now, we will leave you, but I see you. I will come back. Don't bother to see us out, we can find our own way."

* * *

"Where now, boss?" Dan's voice was flattened with disappointment.

"Well, first back to Snow Hill to explain to DCI Parker why all the furore didn't bring us any results. Get on to the team. Bring Kate and Paul up here. I'll organise us somewhere to work. I'm not going back without finding Kayleigh and Jay."

The calls were made, and Tanya was about to call Finch when his caller ID popped up on her tablet screen. "Brian. I was just about to call you. I need Detectives Harris and Lewis up here to assist. Can you hold the fort there?"

"Of course. But I have some information for you."

"Now, is it relevant?" She snapped and then regretted it. No point antagonising him, he could be vindictive at the best of times and this wasn't the best of times.

"Of course, it is. It relates to the weapon. You do remember we are dealing with a murder?"

"Yes, thank you. If I didn't think the situation up here was connected to my case I would be back there. What is it?"

Now he had her defensive. Damn the man.

"Okay, well. Simon Hewitt has examined the knife."

"Oh, you've got it out. Brilliant."

"Of course. It wasn't a problem, just a question of organisation. I had to pull a couple of strings, being the weekend, but it's done. As I say, Simon has had a look and believes it to very possibly be the murder weapon. No chance at all of fingerprints. No chance of DNA…" He held the knife, in the evidence tube, up to the screen of his computer. It was impossible to make out what he was trying to show her. A mixture of light reflection and plastic obscured the visual.

"I can't make it out, Brian. Look I'm really held up here for a while yet. Send me some pictures, will you? I'll come in as soon as I can."

"Do you think maybe you're spreading yourself too thinly? Why don't you concentrate on those youngsters and leave me to deal with things down here? I'm up to date with everything and I can take over easily."

"It's okay, Brian. I've got this. Have you anything more about Sue's accident?"

He didn't want to say anything. She could tell by his face.

"I'm still working on that. I've got it all in hand."

"Oh. So, what's the next move?"

"Just a couple of loose ends to tie up and then I think it'll be sorted. We can't find the other builder. We're looking for him, but he's a casual worker. The site is closed so he's moved on. His car is registered at his brother's address and he hasn't seen him for a while but that's not unusual. He turns up now and then, collects any mail and then he's off again. He sleeps in his van a lot of the time. He's a bit of a loner."

"Have you interviewed the brother?" Tanya asked.

"Not yet, I have that lined up. Tanya. I'm on top of it." But she had the feeling that he was concentrating more on the knife, on the murder. There was so much more kudos in murder than a nasty accident. Before she had a chance to speak, he changed the subject. "How are things going up there?"

"Not good. We still have two missing youngsters."

"Well if I can help, I know people there," he said.

Tanya bit her tongue on the response. *Yes, and they know you.*

She clicked off the tablet and thrust it back into her bag. "Honestly, Dan. It just seems this keeps getting more and more complicated. It's a constant spiral of puzzles and confusion on top of confusion."

"You'll get there, boss. You always do."

She smiled at him. This wasn't the first time he had expressed his absolute faith in her. It was nice, of course it was but, right now, it added to the overwhelming fear of failing everyone.

Chapter 46

By the time Kate and Paul arrived at Snow Hill, Tanya had a room organised and some of the local force co-opted. The atmosphere was tense, nobody was using the few chairs at the front of the room, they gathered towards the back, near the doors. Everyone wanted to get going and find the missing girl.

They had a board with images of Kayleigh and Jayden. Everyone had been given a list of the properties owned by Gregor Belic. Kate handed a sheet to Tanya as they walked into the room.

"This is what we've found so far. He's not been arrested, never been charged with anything but his name pops up all over the place. Drugs – trafficking – and money laundering. Nobody has ever been able to get enough on him to really get close. He's a slippery one and no mistake."

"People trafficking," Tanya said.

"I'm afraid so. It makes it all more urgent, doesn't it?"

Tanya turned to the room. "Okay, we have to find this girl, fast. You will be allocated properties and you go straight there. You tear them apart if you have to. Warrants are in place to search everything this bloke has.

It's not *if* he has her. We know he does. Her brother watched her be driven away. It's where he has her, and why."

One of the local uniformed men held up a hand. "Sorry, ma'am, if we know for sure he has her then why isn't he in custody. Why is he still out there?"

"Good question. The thing is this is all part of a bigger picture. The murder of Carol Barker in Oxford. We have strong reason to suspect the two things are linked. Once we bring him in, the clock starts ticking and he'll have a legal wall around him. I don't believe he will tell us where this girl is and bringing him in may well put her in more danger. I feel our time is better spent, for now at least, looking for her. We are all going out there, I don't want to be sitting in an interview room while you guys are out in the field. We are getting out there, every one of us, and we are looking for these youngsters. There is one property, highlighted. That has already been processed. We know the girl was there, and we think Jayden Gormon was as well – but where are they now? Detective Lewis has more information about this low life, and I want you all to bear it in mind. He's dangerous, he's powerful and he's ruthless – so let's get on with this."

She turned to the sergeant. "Teams of three, please. To each property starting with the nearest to the city centre and working outwards. Everyone keeps us informed. We need to work fast and efficiently. Now, good luck."

The clatter of shoes on the stairs and the slamming of car doors sounded urgent, and watching the cars leaving the car park was reassuring on one level and it was exciting to be a part of. But there was an overriding sense of foreboding as Tanya and Kate set off for their allocated location, a small block of flats converted from a Victorian semi. Dan and Paul had headed for a similar property a few streets away. "This case just keeps getting more and more complicated," Kate said.

"I know. It feels like scattered pieces at the moment. I just hope they all come together soon. Soon enough for us to get this girl home."

"You mean Kayleigh and Jayden, don't you?"

There was a loaded silence.

"I have a bad feeling about Jayden. There must be a reason Carl thinks he's dead. We haven't been able to pin him down on it. He says he doesn't know, but something has made him think that. His mum is lovely, she's had a rough ride and, okay, she's probably made some mistakes with him but she loves him, and she wants him home. I want him home…"

There was no need to say more.

* * *

The property was shabby-looking and down at heel. The front door needed painting and the garden was just a patch of weedy grass with a sad shrub growing against the wall. The windows needed cleaning and the gate hung on one hinge.

"He's not much of a landlord, is he?" Kate said.

"No, but it's all handled through an agent, so one removed. He just takes the money."

Tanya hammered on the front door and they both took a pace backwards looking up at the grubby windows. A large bloke wearing a loose Hawaiian shirt and a pair of floppy grey shorts eventually answered the door.

Tanya waved the warrant at him. "We have a warrant to search these premises. Please go to your own rooms. We will want to speak to you shortly."

They pushed past him to knock on the door to the ground floor flat. They went into three of the four small apartments. The fourth was empty. Tanya made a call to get a locksmith out to gain entrance. They interviewed the residents. Nobody knew anything, nobody had seen anything. No new noises, no new tenants. She knew there was nothing there. It was just cheap housing with innocent people trying to get by.

By the time they had finished the interviews, the last flat was open. It was furnished cheaply. A couple of settees from Ikea, a double bed and chipboard wardrobe in the one bedroom and old battered units in the tiny kitchen. The place smelled of damp and felt empty. "Nobody has been in here. We aren't going to find anything. Come on Kate, let's get on to the next one."

They left their cards with the tenants and a request they be called if anything happened they should know about. They knew it was a waste of time.

Kate ticked off the address on her sheet and began to programme the sat nav for the next destination. Tanya's phone rang. She didn't recognise the number.

"Miller."

"Hello. My mum said I had to ring you."

"Who is this?"

"My name's Kayleigh. My mum said I had to ring you."

Tanya reached out and grabbed Kate's arm. "Where are you?"

"I'm at home. What have you done with my brother?"

Chapter 47

As Tanya and Kate drew up at the kerb, the door to the Grants' house opened. Frances Grant waited until they were halfway down the path and then she stepped back inside leaving the detectives to follow her.

Kayleigh was curled on the sofa, legs tucked under her. She was wrapped in a thin dressing gown and sipping at a mug of tea. She looked up as they entered the room but didn't make any attempt to stand.

Tanya perched at the other end of the settee. "I'm DI Miller, this is DC Kate Lewis. Are you okay, Kayleigh? We've been really worried about you. There've been a lot of people out trying to find you. We're relieved you're back. Do you want to tell us what happened?"

"Nothing happened. Why have you arrested my brother?"

"Carl hasn't been arrested, Kayleigh. He's just helping us with some enquiries. He was really upset and worried about you. Do you need a doctor?"

"No! I don't need a doctor. Why would I need a doctor? I reckon you can just let Carl come home now. He got the wrong idea. I'm fine."

"You've got a couple of bruises there on your arms, Kayleigh. How did you get those?" Kate asked.

The girl pulled down the sleeve of her dressing gown. "They're nothing. Just larking about."

"Where did Gregor take you?" As she asked the question Tanya pulled out her mobile phone. "You don't mind if I record this, do you? Just to make sure we have it straight."

"Knock yourself out. I haven't got anything to say, anyway. I don't know what all the fuss is about."

"We were under the impression you were held against your will, locked in an industrial unit and then taken away in a car by Mr Belic."

"Don't know where you got that from. I went for a ride, yes. Just out to one of his houses. There was a bit of a party. We just hung out."

"Who did?"

"Me and some other girls. Girls who work in his club. They were nice. We just watched some movies. Had a couple of drinks. Just alcopops, nothing heavy."

"Where was this?" The girl shook her head. "Dunno, never been there before."

"And how did you get back here?"

"One of the blokes dropped me off in town. I got the train. I'm fine. Carl's got it all wrong. There's no problem." As she spoke her gaze flicked constantly between her mother and Tanya. Frances was silent, watchful. The shivering and twitching had stopped, she looked calm. It was obvious she'd had something that had eased her craving.

"Will you not let us get you a doctor? Just to make sure you're okay." Kate was using what Tanya thought of as her 'mummy' voice, but it did no good. Kayleigh slammed the cup down onto the table.

"I told you. I'm okay. I don't need anything but Carl back here. You can let him come home now. It's all been a mistake."

"No, we can't just now. Did you see Jayden at this house?"

"Jay. No – I haven't seen Jay for ages. No, he wasn't there."

As she answered Kayleigh turned away, she chewed at her bottom lip and started picking at the buttons on the front of her robe. Tanya took one of her cards from her pocket, held it out to the girl.

"Take this. If you change your mind, if you want to talk to me, or Detective Lewis, you can call us at any time. We know you're worried. We think you've been scared but there's no need. We can help you. Just let us help you."

* * *

Back in the car Tanya leaned her forehead against the steering wheel. "Well, he's got to her good and proper, hasn't he? She's scared stiff."

"Yes. We're not going to get anything out of her. Did you notice the mother? She'd had a fix. That was probably part of the bargain. So, where does this leave us?"

"Absolutely bloody nowhere." Tanya slipped the car into gear and pulled into the road. She drove in silence for a while.

"We're going to hand Carl over to the local drug team. With luck they'll maybe get him to help them nail Gregor. We'll give them all the help we can, but this is theirs now. There are still teams out looking for Jayden. We can't prove Gregor had him. Maybe he didn't, maybe he's buggered off to London. I've got him on the Misper list and reports are coming in from the property searches, they haven't found any sign of him. There's also no place where there are girls from his club, though the club has been searched. He has places we don't know about, obviously. Again, that has to be left up to the locals."

"So, you don't have him down for the murder, Gregor I mean?"

"Not this particular time, no. It doesn't feel right. Why would he kill her if Mrs Barker was under his control? He'd lose the drop. Okay, Carl said she was always trying to make them stop, to leave her alone, but she hadn't, had she? She hadn't called us. She hadn't told her daughter. I think the poor woman was just too scared to do anything. Maybe she hoped she could convince the boys to help her get out of the mess she was in. Maybe she tried to use her experience as a teacher. But it didn't work. She was trapped, vulnerable and alone. She'd been bullied and scared into letting them use her house to store the drugs and then hold the money until it was collected. She didn't understand that it wasn't kids she was dealing with, at least not the sort she was used to. It was much bigger than that and really the boys were as trapped as she was in the whole filthy business. She couldn't speak to their parents, contact their school, all the things that she would have done years ago. They weren't even the children she'd been teaching. They were sent from another city altogether. She must have been so confused by it all. Anyway, we should look at the rival drugs gangs. I think Gregor is as puzzled as we are about what's happened. I reckon if he knew, we would have had a genuine turf war on our hands. He took Carl, maybe Jayden, he wouldn't have done that if he'd killed her himself, would he? They were useful assets, already under his control. He won't want to act unless he's sure of what's going on, and I don't think he's sure. Tell you what, Kate, are you up to driving for a bit? I'm absolutely whacked, and I need to review my messages. And make the calls."

"Of course, boss. Next services we'll swap over. Are you okay? I mean I get you're tired but there's nothing else, is there?"

"Frustration and, okay, worry. Bob Scunthorpe is going to be needing an explanation about all of this and right now, I don't know what I'm going to tell him."

They swapped in the car park at the services and Kate ran in to bring them coffee. Once they were back on the carriageway, she left Tanya to work. They drove on as the sun went down in front of them, lights on the passing cars made jewelled necklaces stretching for miles. There was nothing in the car but the tap of Tanya's fingers on the virtual keyboard and then a few short telephone calls and FaceTime with DCI Parker. It was a strange sort of peace after the frenetic pace of the last few days.

"Okay. I've cleared the decks. We'll liaise closely with Snow Hill, but right now we can do more good back home. At least Finch has had some success. He's found what we believe is the murder weapon. How much help it's going to be, dug out from wet concrete, I don't know. We'll shift our attention back to the original scene. We've been led down a dead end and it's my fault. I need to sort it pretty bloody quickly."

The next time Kate looked across the car, Tanya's eyes were closed; her breathing was slow and deep.

Chapter 48

It was late evening by the time they arrived back in Oxford. The station was quiet. Up in their shared office, Brian Finch was packing to leave. "Oh, I thought you'd changed your mind. Gone straight home," he said.

"Why would you think that? I said I'd be back in. Have you got the knife? The pictures weren't a lot of use."

"No, well I couldn't take it out of the case. It's here. I was just about to check it back in to evidence."

He handed over the plastic tube holding the knife. "No fingerprints then?" Tanya asked.

"No. There are a couple of suspicious-looking stains on the handle. We thought they might be blood, but even if they are, forensics reckon they won't be any use for DNA because of the concrete and what have you. I had a word with them about it."

Tanya reached and took the container from him. She held it to the light, peering in at the dirty blade and the black plastic handle. "Yes, I see where you mean. The lab hasn't had it yet then?"

Brian shook his head. "First job tomorrow."

She tipped the tube and held it closer to the light. "It looks pretty average."

"Yes, you can buy them at fishing shops, even some market stalls. It's nothing special I'm afraid," Brian said.

"And the scratches?" Tanya said.

"Sorry?"

"These scratches, on the blade just under the handle. Have we any idea what they are?"

"It's pretty beaten up. Not surprising given we had to dig it out of a concrete block."

"Yeah, of course I get that. But these ones, by the handle. They look deliberate. What have you done about those? Have we got close-ups of them?"

Brian looked at her in silence. "I've been busy," he said. "I had that here waiting for you, but I've been doing other work. I'm writing my report on the accident, being thorough."

"So, you haven't seen these?"

He sighed and moved closer so, when she tipped the tube, he could see more clearly. "Oh those. Yes, I saw them, but I didn't think they were anything to make a fuss about."

So, now he was accusing her of making a fuss.

"Well, Brian – I don't agree. To me they look as though they could have been done deliberately. They appear to have been scratched into the metal rather than simply being the result of wear and tear. Not only that but, in my opinion, I think they might be initials. If they are then the murderer has very likely left us his autograph. Leave this with me. I reckon they'll be able to enhance these. They must have a way to do that. I'll speak to them first thing in the morning."

"I signed it out. I'll deal with it."

"No, it's fine, Brian. You get off home. I'll take it back now and then tomorrow I'll get the lab onto this."

He glared at her. Snorted down his nose, but he had no real choice other than to turn and stomp out of the office. Tanya leaned closer into the lamp. She didn't want to be wrong, not least because if she was, he would make sure everyone knew. But more than that, this could be huge, and right now she needed something huge. She pulled a magnifying glass out of the desk drawer and spent a while peering at the knife. She wanted to take it out, but the tube was sealed, and Brian had signed it out of storage. The risk of interrupting the chain of evidence was too great. When it became obvious all she had was a bigger, blurrier view of the scratches, she had to give it up and take it back to the evidence room.

She had felt refreshed after her short snooze in the car but now the lack of sleep caught up with her again and she went home.

After a large whisky and a warm shower, she slid into bed. Her brain began to re-run the events of the day, the worries about Jayden Gormon, Carl and Kayleigh and Sue. She couldn't shake the feeling that his original investigation was being side-lined. Finch had let his attention be drawn to the other case. It wasn't right. It wasn't fair. In the end exhaustion won the fight, and in the early hours of the morning she slept at last.

* * *

Back in Birmingham, Carl lay awake in the detention centre. At home, his mother sprawled on the settee lost in a fug of booze and drugs while her daughter cried up in her bedroom and dabbed witch hazel on the bruises. She made an online appointment with the nurse at the GP practice. She needed to get the morning after pill, just in case. She stood in the shower for the third time that evening and let the hot water sooth the sore spots and wash away the filth, but she knew nothing would ever wash away the brutality of what had happened to her.

Chapter 49

Tanya was in the office by six the next morning. Kate wasn't long behind her.

"Bruises are fading," Tanya said.

"Yes. I toyed with the idea of make-up again, but it just made me look odd. I'm not good with all that stuff. Anyway, nobody looks at me."

"Oh, come on. You look really good…" Tanya stopped.

Kate grinned at her. "For my age?"

"No, that's not what I was going to say. Well, you do of course but – I…"

Kate turned away with a laugh.

They updated the board, moving the images of Carl, his sister and Jayden to the outside. Gregor was there with a large question mark over the image. Tanya stood back. "We know they're all connected but what I don't get is why they would kill her. If the boys had stolen Gregor's drugs or his money and made a run for it then, maybe. If she had tried to fight back, maybe. But it doesn't fit with what's happened since. So, it's got to be someone else. We'll keep in close touch with Birmingham, but I just feel this has all become peripheral. I don't know where that leaves us. Well, I do. It leaves us pretty much nowhere."

"I had a word with a friend in Organised Crime yesterday. As far as they're aware there's no sort of feud or gang thing going on. I have to say they were grateful for the information we have about Gregor. They hadn't got him on their radar for our area. I put them in touch with Snow Hill. We'll hear immediately if anything pops up relating back to Mrs Barker but for the moment it's just another 'County Lines' case to add to the others they're dealing with. On the upside the more people looking at our nice Mr Belic the better and especially if it leads us to Jayden," Kate said.

"Okay, back to Mrs Barker. The knife. I've arranged for it to go to the lab as soon as possible this morning. I'm hoping they'll be able to get a clearer image of the scratches. I'm convinced they're initials. Look." She held out a print. "What do you think?"

Kate screwed up her eyes and then leaned over to her desk to pick up the glasses she used when she was working with the computer. "Maybe an eight, the first one. I think the second one is an A and then perhaps a zero. But it doesn't mean anything, does it?"

"Think of letters rather than numbers. I mean, the only reason I can think you would do that would be to put your name on it."

Kate nodded. "Yeah, that makes sense. So, it's got to be a B doesn't it – or possibly an S, one of the curly ones at least, and the last one could be an O. We'll stick this on the board and when the team get in maybe we can all have a go and see what we come up with. If the lab sends us something clearer, perhaps we won't have to guess."

"Keep on at them, Kate. It's all there is, and I have a meeting with DCI Scunthorpe later. If they are initials, they're not Carl's though, are they? Not Jayden's or of course Gregor's. I suppose it could be one of his thugs," Tanya said. "We'll just have to wait."

Kate collected their coffee cups and the greasy napkins from breakfast. The building was coming to life and it wouldn't be long before the room was filled.

"Has DI Finch written his report about Sue's accident?" Kate asked.

"He said he was working on it yesterday. It worries me though."

"Do you want to share?"

"No, I don't want it to become the subject of rumour and conjecture, I don't want to put the cat among the pigeons."

Kate waited for a while in silence, obviously she was hoping to be told more but it was Brian's bag and Tanya knew he'd want the credit. She didn't care. As long as they did justice to the investigation, that was what mattered.

She went through to the office and watched the footage again. She saw now what it was that had been niggling at her. Every time it was more convincing, clearer. Sue was speaking to someone. As soon as Brian came in, she was going to have a word. Maybe he'd let her have a look at his report. She needed to know he'd emphasised this because it was important and she didn't want it pushed aside because it would draw things out, cost more money and time. She took out the statements and started to read through them again. She was so totally lost in the accounts of what had happened, Kate had to come and find her. "We're ready, boss. Everyone's in."

Now she had to go and address the team and all she had to give them were more puzzles, no progress. She had to try and do it in a way that didn't show she had no idea where to look next.

"I'm going back to the house later today. I'm going back to the beginning because I want to clarify my thinking. Dan, you're with me. The rest of you…" She paused. She knew they had been peering at screens for hours but so much of it had been for next to nothing now they had handed over the drug investigation to

Birmingham. "I want you going through it all from the start. We've missed something here and we need to find it." She turned away from the looks of frustration and disappointment on their faces but just before she left the room she stopped. She walked over to the board and pointed at the picture of Carol Barker under the tree. "I know this is slow, I know it seems as though we've got nowhere but this woman was killed in cold blood. Someone came into her home, where she should have been safe, and took her life. I want you telephoning the neighbours, I want you going through the statements. Anything at all you think might help us to find the thread. It's there and it's going to unravel if we just keep pulling."

As she walked down the corridor she cringed. *Unravel if we just keep pulling.* Had she really just said that?

"Boss!" Kate was leaning out of the office door. "Picture from the lab. They've done a great job. We can see the letters much more clearly." Tanya turned and ran back. "It's a word, boss," Kate said. "I don't know it's going to be much help. It just says SAD."

"Sad," Tanya repeated. "Okay. I want any and all ideas. Why would you write that on a knife blade? Is it gang related? Kate, get some people researching it: knife crime, gang slogans, even killers who have used knives, see if they scratched words into their blades. It's all we've got. It has to mean something." She sounded confident but her stomach felt hollowed out. This could just be some silly quirk of the owner's, a casual scribble made to pass the time, it could mean absolutely nothing.

Chapter 50

"Take your own car, would you, Dan." As they left the car park, Tanya dialled Charlie's number up in Liverpool. She would just let it ring a few times, he was probably working.

"Hi, this is a surprise. Are you on leave? Do NOT tell me you've got yourself injured again."

"No, no. I'm okay. Are you busy?"

"On a break right now, just paperwork at the mo. Are you okay, Tanya? You sound a bit down."

Now she was talking to him, she didn't really know why she had called. This wasn't her, she was a loner, resilient. "I'm sorry, Charlie. I don't know why I rang really. It's just this case."

"Still not broken it open yet?"

"No, I'm going round in circles. Every lead turns into a dead end, every trail I follow just throws up another problem, and there's Sue."

"Yes. Well, to be honest I reckon it's probably most of your problem, mate."

"How do you mean?"

"Come on, Tanya. She was one of your team. She was working with you. Now, she's dead. You can't just shrug this stuff off. I know you're tough, but you are also human. Give yourself a break."

"Ha. That sounds like a pep talk."

"Well, that's because it is. Don't be so hard on yourself. You'll get there. You always do. Just keep on working at it."

"I'm trying to. Listen, one thing. I've got a knife with something scratched on the blade. I'm thinking maybe gangland?"

"Yeah, possible, like tattoos or clothes. Then there's the Knife Angel, isn't there?"

"The what?"

"It was a sculpture made of thousands of knives. It was to draw attention to knife crime. Those blades had personal messages engraved on them. It wasn't every force but quite a number were involved. What was it on your blade?"

"It's not really a message. Looks like a word – Sad."

"Hmm – maybe someone wanted to surrender the knife. That was the whole idea. An amnesty. Then they found out that wasn't the way it worked. Perhaps they liked the idea of their words on the statue. But the messages on the blades were from victims' families so they changed their minds. It's tenuous but it might be worth keeping in mind."

"I don't think I knew about that, Charlie – what was it again?"

"The Knife Angel. It's on the web. Sorry, T, I have to go. Call me again later. Don't be so hard on yourself."

"Thanks, Charlie." As he ended the call, she realised she'd forgotten to ask about the baby. She'd ring him again later. She called Kate and asked her to research the Knife Angel. It might be nothing, but it was worth looking into. Anything was worth looking into.

* * *

They walked around the house again. It told them nothing new except it was sadder, dustier, and the food in the fridge was going to need throwing away soon. Tanya remembered when Kate was keen on having the place cleaned. It was just before she was whacked in the face with a backpack. "Dan. When we get back, could you have one of the civilians contact Stella Barker? Find out if she wants someone to come in and sort this place out. I reckon we've finished with it now and a cleaning company could make it more presentable."

"Yes, boss. No problem." She knew he was staring at her, but she carried on walking out into the back garden.

"Every time I see this place I wonder why. Why did she run into a closed space? It doesn't make sense."

"Maybe she thought she could attract the attention of a neighbour."

"But she was bleeding, dying. How was she going to do that? She didn't scream, or if she did nobody heard her. Could it be she knew the boys were coming? Carl said they came over the fence, '*the same as always.*' If he was telling the truth could it be that she was expecting them and hoped they would help her? If that's the case, maybe it's what scared the killer away. If he heard them, saw them, and just ran. Of course, that would mean it was nothing to do with the drugs. It wasn't as Carl and Jayden feared, that the killer might be waiting for them. He never intended them harm. Maybe he was shocked and scared. It puts a different light on things. After all this, it could be that it was simply a robbery gone wrong."

"But there was money in her purse. Jewellery in the drawers upstairs, computers, some silver on the sideboard."

"Well, yes, but as I said, maybe it just went wrong and he didn't get anything. No, no it just doesn't work, the disturbance looked like a struggle not a burglary. I still think he came to kill."

Chapter 51

"Come on down to the building site, Dan. I want to have a look at where the knife was."

The house was still taped off but there was no longer anyone in uniform at the gate. The concrete had been a smooth new pathway and it was destroyed, piles of rubble on the grass beside it.

Dan glanced up at the broken scaffolding. "This must be frustrating for the builders. Any idea how long before we have the final report on the accident?"

"Might not be as straightforward as it seemed, Dan. I don't want to say too much right now, but it looks like there's a complication." As she spoke, they were both aware of movement at the back of the house. "Hello. Who's there?"

"Could ask you the same question. What are you doing in here? Ghouls are you, rubberneckers? Oh, it's you. Aren't you that policewoman?"

"DI Tanya Miller. We've met before, I think."

"Aye. I'm George. What are you doing here now? Don't tell me there's sommat else. Haven't you caused enough trouble?" He kicked at the ruined path. "You lot have really screwed up this bloody job, good and proper."

"What exactly are you doing here, Mr Roberts?" Tanya asked.

"Just keeping an eye on stuff. We've got tools here, supplies. You can't turn your back without somebody nicking things, filling your skips with rubbish, what have you. Somebody needs to check on it all. This is costing my gaffer a fortune, all of this delay."

"Sorry about that but we're working as fast as we can to find out what's gone on here. We are also trying to find your mate. Stewart, was it?"

"Aye well. Good luck. He's buggered off with a bag full of tools as well. Haven't seen him. Mind you, nothing for him to do, is there? I've told my boss over and over. These casuals are a risk. Some of 'em are okay but what I say is if a bloke wants to work in construction there's ways to do it. It's easy, government grants for study and what have you, help from the job seekers' thing, but no. Thinks it makes sense because he doesn't have to pay for their stamp. Well he's made off with a damn site more than the cost of his National Insurance now."

"Have you reported it?" Dan said.

"Ha. Don't be so bloody daft."

"What do you know about him, this Stewart?" Tanya asked.

"Dead loss. A bit thick. A grumpy sod, actually. Lives in his van. He was pretty strong and worked hard enough, I'll give him that."

"Right, thanks. That's incredibly helpful."

He picked up the sarcasm and in truth Tanya had made no attempt to hide it.

"My pleasure," he grunted. He turned away, spat onto the path, and then stomped back to the rear of the property.

"Well, we might as well go. You saw the pictures of the bloke burying the knife?" Tanya spoke, quietly, almost musing. Dan had to lean in to listen. "At first we thought it was one of the boys."

"Yes, but it's been debunked, hasn't it? The report from Birmingham said his trainers were clean. They were the only pair he had and there was no sign of mud or concrete dust in the treads. No mud or blood on the uppers. It's still possible but it's looking less likely. Why, what are you thinking?"

"Well, as you say it is looking less likely now he had anything to do with the killing. He's in enough trouble though. But that builder we've just been talking to" – Tanya nodded towards the house – "he was wearing big heavy boots. Probably the ones with steel in the toes. They were filthy, weren't they? Covered in building grime."

"Yes. Where are you going with this?"

"Bear with me. So, if you worked on a site regularly, you'd have the gear, wouldn't you? Or if you were a permanent employee, you'd maybe be issued with them by the company. But if you were casual labour, perhaps short of cash or the boss was trying to save money, well maybe you'd just wear what you had. Let's get back, Dan. We'll have another look. We'll run the original CCTV footage."

As they turned away, Tanya felt the little flutter of excitement in her gut. Something had just fallen into place. She didn't have a complete hold on it yet, but the vibe had altered. The mist was clearing, she could feel it.

In the office they played the film, freezing it at the best view of the feet.

"Look, his jeans are dirty, the hems and up on the fronts. Can we zoom in? I want the closest view of his hands and arms we can get. I want a still of them. If I'm right those won't be a young lad's hands at all. They'll be a man's hands. Someone who does manual work. Maybe like on a building site." She turned to Dan and raised her eyebrows.

"Bloody hell."

"If I hadn't been flying around the country chasing kids, I would have paid better attention to this. I left too much to other people and screwed up."

Chapter 52

They ran the film a couple of times. Kate and Paul crowded in to see over their shoulders and by the end they were convinced. These were not the hands of a young boy. They were bigger, muscular. "Look at the way he moves," Tanya said, "and later, look at how he smooths down the concrete, using that piece of wood. He's done that before. A young lad wouldn't know how to do it, well probably not. Okay it's spoiled, not quite as smooth, but only because we know what we're looking for."

"Why the hell didn't we pick up on this?" Tanya growled.

"DI Finch viewed it, boss. He put stills up on the board, that was all. It was all about the trainers and the concrete. We didn't know what he was doing. He was keeping it all pretty much under wraps. He said he wanted the investigation into Sue's accident to be totally independent. All just flannel if you ask me. Sorry, boss, that was out of line."

Tanya lowered her head for a minute to hide the grin, took in a deep breath and then stood. "Right. This is my fault, nobody else's. I should have taken more notice."

The others didn't answer. They knew, all of them. Brian Finch hadn't seen the importance of what he was looking at. Yes, the knife had been a massive breakthrough but, in the excitement, he had failed to take in the detail. He had done a sloppy job and made assumptions. Because of that, hours, maybe days had been lost.

Eventually, Paul muttered low, under his breath, "Should have been highlighted."

Tanya stared at him, daring him to say more. He turned away.

"Right, I'll get on to the DVLA. We need the licence plate for the ANPR cameras. We need to know where this van is."

His action broke the mood and the others went back to their desks. "I've got the address of the brother. He's in Headington, I think. Quarter of an hour. Do you want to go now, boss?" Kate said.

"Too bloody true, I do. Dan, come with me, will you? The rest of you follow up on the ANPR. If he is seen, let me know straight away."

* * *

The address was in an affluent suburb within the Oxford Brookes University Campus. The house they were looking for was a semi, built early in the twentieth century. There was a neat garden, blinds at the windows, it was well cared for. A VW Arteon, just two years old, was parked outside. When Tanya touched the bonnet, it was warm under her hand. "Well, the brother's doing okay," Dan said. "These houses are not cheap."

"And yet, his sibling is living in a van somewhere. Families, eh!"

The doorbell was answered by a tall, middle-aged man in suit trousers and formal shirt with a zip up hoodie over the top. "No thank you. I don't want to change my energy supplier, sign up for faster broadband, and I'm not interested in Jehovah."

He began to push the door closed and Tanya reached out to lay a hand on the wood. He raised his eyebrows.

"Don't do that. Look, I don't want to be rude, but I've just got in from work. I'm tired and I need a G and T so – go away."

By this time Dan had pulled out his warrant card and Tanya pushed her hand into her pocket to extract her own wallet.

"Oh." Now the door was opened wider. "Sorry. I didn't know."

They confirmed his name, Anthony. "Please call me Tony."

"May we come in for a minute? It shouldn't take long," Tanya said.

"Of course. What's the problem? It's not Sylvia, is it?"

"Sylvia?"

"My ex. She's up in Manchester right now. She's okay, isn't she?"

"As far as we know. There's nothing to be alarmed about, Mr Dawes. We have a few questions regarding your brother. Stewart."

There was a noticeable change in his demeanour and, as he stepped away from the door, they saw his shoulders slump. "Right. Okay, what's happened now?"

They followed him through the hallway into a square kitchen at the back of the house. There was a ready meal defrosting on the worktop and a tall glass of gin and tonic on the table. Ice from a tray had melted and Tony Dawes grabbed a cloth to clean up the puddle.

"When did you last see your brother, Mr Dawes?" Dan asked.

The other man blew out his cheeks and let out a puff of air through pursed lips.

"Oh, I guess it was about three weeks ago, something like that. He was in the area and came to borrow some money."

He picked up the drink and took a big gulp. "It's okay. I don't mind. He has problems and I try to help him out. I feel guilty because, well, I promised our mum I'd look after him. I know she meant I should have him live with me after she died. But I just can't. He's…" There was a moment while he searched for the word. "He's difficult and disruptive. Not all the time, just now and then. He can't help it."

"How do you mean, difficult?" Tanya had taken out her notebook and was jotting in it as she spoke.

"He has anger issues. I think that's the way we're supposed to refer to it now. Back in the day I guess we'd have said he was a bad-tempered sod. He's not dangerous or anything. Not these days anyway. When he was younger it was different. He was out of control some of the time then but nowadays, as long as he takes his medication, he's fine. He's been away for the last few years. France, Germany. He likes to move around. We speak on the phone now and then. I send him money if he gets desperate. I'll be honest, I don't want him back in my life full time. I gave him money and let him sleep here a couple of nights. That was all. We're not close, not really."

"Where does he live?" Dan asked.

"Nowhere permanent. He takes on casual work. Seasonal stuff sometimes, fruit picking and what have you."

"Labouring?" Tanya said.

"Yeah. All those sorts of thing. He does his best. I only let him stay a day or two. He didn't really give me any choice. Well, I couldn't let him sleep on the streets, could I?" Tony paused and took another gulp of his drink. "I work in town. Insurance, investments. He turned up outside the office. I can't have that."

He waited for them to speak. He was embarrassed and awkward. Tanya understood about family problems. "Nobody is judging you, Mr Dawes."

"Thank you. I feel bad. Mum would have been disappointed in me and I wanted to help him but I like my life. I've been through a couple of bad years with the divorce. Then, just when things were starting to settle, Stew turned up. Look, I did what I could. I bought him a van. That's how come it's registered here. It's done out so he can sleep in it. He likes to move about. I thought it would be okay. Why do you need to speak to him?"

"I'd rather not get into that just now."

"He hasn't had an accident, has he?"

"Not as far as we are aware, no," Dan said.

"Did you grow up around here, Mr Dawes?"

"Yes, well sort of. Over in Summertown. I moved when I went to uni. Mum and Dad moved…" He paused. "Well, they moved when Stewart was expelled from school."

"Why was he expelled?" Tanya said.

"It was a misunderstanding. He was accused of bullying. There were a couple of incidents and him being the way he is…" He shrugged. "A boy was hurt. Hurt quite badly. He lost the sight in one eye. Afterwards it was horrible for Mum and Dad. People shunned them. Said they should have him locked up. Anyway, it's a long time ago now. Stewart never really got over it. He liked school, he had plans, university and what have you. He wanted to be an architect. He'd done well in his exams and been accepted at his first choice. Anyway, afterwards none of it was possible and he just sort of gave up. Then he went abroad. He was bitter, depressed for a while. Blamed the school, the education system, mainly he blamed the teachers. Everyone but himself. He's just angry. Well it's a bitter tale and best forgotten."

"Was the school Saint Matthews?" Tanya said.

"Yes, it was. How did you know?"

"Oh. Just a guess."

She had felt Dan tense beside her and knew he had picked up on the name.

"Do you have any of his things, from when he stayed with you?" Tanya asked.

"How do you mean?"

"His hairbrush, toothbrush, anything like that. Personal things."

"I don't think so. Well, I don't know. He stayed in the guest room. It has an en-suite bathroom. I could have a look."

"Has anyone else used the room since he was here?"

"No. Nobody."

"So, if there is a toothbrush or anything, it would be his?" Tanya said.

"Well, sort of. I keep a couple of cheap ones in case I have someone staying over unexpectedly. Do you want me to look?"

"Please. And if you let Detective Constable Price come with you and take anything you think might have been his, we'd be grateful."

"This is something serious, isn't it? You're looking for DNA, aren't you? Has he hurt someone?"

"Why do you ask, sir?"

"As I say, he has a temper. He isn't always in control. Oh God, what has he done?"

"We don't know if he's done anything. We would just like to eliminate him from our enquiries."

They could tell from the look on his face, he didn't believe them.

Chapter 53

Back in the office Tanya mobilised the team. "I want you, Kate, to find out all you can about this incident at the school. If the boy was badly hurt there'll be something in the papers or online. We need to find this bloke. I don't like coincidences. He attended the school Mrs Barker taught at. She was his form mistress. We looked at the leavers' book his brother had, she held up the hard-backed volume. I have it here. Of course, Stewart Dawes isn't in it. The injured boy is. You can pick him out immediately." She pointed to a class picture with one boy wearing dark glasses, a scar across his forehead. "Paul, get his address, go and see him, find out whether he's had any problems. At this point I don't think we need to trace all the classmates, but that might come later. The teachers should be approached. The headmaster. We need to trace Mr Dawes as a matter of urgency."

They made good progress and by ten o'clock Tanya decided they had achieved all they reasonably could. There was still no news on the van, but if he was sleeping in it, then it could be parked up somewhere obscure. The word was out, she would keep her fingers crossed. Sometimes it was luck with something like this. An astute uniformed officer, a patrol car in the right place at the right time but if not, then they would have him as soon as he drove on a major road. She had to be patient.

They called it a day.

* * *

Mrs Green had been in and everywhere smelled of polish and floor cleaner. There was a dish on the table covered in foil. A sticky note told her it was *Just a bit of a chicken casserole. Pop it in the oven for half an hour. There's no food in the fridge – AGAIN'*. She was a genuine treasure.

While she waited for the food to warm, Tanya opened the inevitable white envelope, another bank letter. They were going to stop her Direct Debit payments unless she cleared the unagreed part of her overdraft. She looked down at the dish in the oven. If they did, she would have to pay Mrs Green in cash. She didn't have any cash. She was going to have to sort this. But not now, not tonight, not with chicken casserole to eat and white wine to drink. Tomorrow she would find a way to deal with it. Maybe Fiona would help her out. She had paid her back for the last loan – hadn't she? Surely. She should have slept well, the case had begun to make some sense, she was convinced of it. But her dreams were of cash just out of reach, her house crumbling around her. A vile and greedy bank manager laughing as he tore up all her clothes. In the end she woke at five, had a long hot shower and went into work.

* * *

By the time she had the call from DI Scunthorpe, two cups of strong coffee and a sugar hit from the box of doughnuts Dan brought in had her in a much better place.

"Tanya. You look tired."

It wasn't quite the greeting she was expecting and left her floundering for words.

"I'm fine, sir. Really. It's been a bit hectic but, I'm okay."

"Take care of yourself, Inspector. I can't afford to lose more manpower." She wasn't sure whether that was a direct reference to Sue or a general comment on the manning issues plaguing the service countrywide.

"First of all, I have received communication from Snow Hill. They wanted me to pass on their congratulations and thanks. Your investigation has given them vital information. They are hopeful they'll be able to build a strong case against Gregor Belic. They've been struggling with it a bit, he's well protected, but the young man…"

He glanced at the file in front of him.

"Carl Grant is being very helpful. Of course, they'll be organising some sort of a deal with him, but they reckon it's going to be worth it. He's already given them several other addresses they were using as drops. There's another elderly woman, a boy with learning difficulties who is trying to be independent, a single mother who is an addict. They have already taken away her baby for safety. It's so cruel, this thing. Anyway, because of what you've done they can shut down this low life, at least for a while."

"That's good to hear, sir. Is there any news about the other boy – Jayden Gormon?"

"Nothing. The general consensus seems to be he has gone to ground. Maybe in London. We have him in the Misper list and we'll just have to hope for the best."

"I felt bad for his mother that we weren't able to find him. I think it may be a good idea for someone to have another word with Kayleigh Grant. Now she's had a few days. I didn't buy her story that nothing had happened to her."

"Yes, they have passed that to the relevant unit already, but you know the problems there. If she won't talk, there's not much anyone can do. Tanya, you have to leave it to Birmingham. They are perfectly able to conduct their own enquiries. I understand you feel a sense of responsibility, but you must let it go. However, it's a feather in your cap that you have done what you have. Congratulations. Now then. What about our own case, this murder? I think it best you concentrate on that."

A day earlier and this would have been an embarrassing question but now she felt so much more confident. She smiled. "I think we may have made a breakthrough there." She told him of the developments.

"I'm not sure I follow you."

"We have ascertained Mrs Barker was working in the school at the same time as Stewart Dawes had his problems. He threatened the school staff who were involved in the investigation with repercussions after he was expelled. Now, as far as we have been able to find out there have been no attacks on anyone else. We are in the early stages of our research. But he has lived away from Oxford for the last few years only returning to visit his brother recently. I have the team working on this, sir. We will find him."

"Let's do it before we have another attack."

"Yes, sir, that is definitely our aim. We are tracing the people involved. We will keep them informed and find out if any of them has been approached or had anything happen to concern them. Three of them are retired and one has died of natural causes. We need to find him quickly, sir, and we will."

"Well done, Tanya. Keep me informed."

"Sir, there is something else."

Scunthorpe nodded; raised his eyebrows.

"Has DI Finch been to see you, sir? About DC Rollinson's accident."

"I have an appointment with him later. Representatives of the Health and Safety Executive are to attend. I'm hoping we'll be able to put that to bed as well. All in all, a good day, yes?"

She had to tell him, didn't she? "There has been a development, sir."

Bob Scunthorpe sighed, he pushed the file to one side and folded his hands on the desktop. "I'm not going to be happy, am I?"

"Probably not, sir."

"Okay. Out with it."

"There is the possibility there was someone on the scaffolding above where DC Rollinson-Bakshi was standing." She didn't need to say anymore.

"How sure are you?"

"Pretty sure, sir."

"Right. You realise this is a real spanner in the works. If someone was there and they haven't come forward, then it points to this being at the least a cover-up by the company."

"Yes, sir."

"I need to see the footage. Now. Arrange it, will you, and don't leave the building until I have had a chance to view it."

So much for looking tired and taking care of herself. As she left his office Tanya glanced at her watch. It was already after ten. If they traced the van, they would be out on the road again. This other thing was Brian Finch's job. There was no choice but to do as she was told. The walk down the corridor was the nearest thing to a jog as was possible without actually breaking into a run. Brian was going to be livid. She smiled.

Chapter 54

Tanya barged into the office.

"Right, everybody – can I have your attention? Are you all up to date with this new development?" She pointed to the image of Stewart Dawes which had been pinned on the board. There was a mumble of assent.

"We need to find him. I think we need to find him quickly. He made threats, okay they were made some time ago and I think it's safe to say nobody took them very seriously. Over time they have been all but forgotten, but now I think he is following up on them." She turned to Kate. "Has the observation been set up on the teachers?"

"Yes, boss. We have also alerted the school. None of the teachers who were involved originally are still there, but we have cars passing their houses regularly and they have been given emergency contact numbers. The current head of the school has been informed and has briefed his own security."

"His own security?" Tanya said.

"Yes, boss, they have patrols at night in case of arson attacks, robbery, vandalism, and during the day they have a bouncer on the door."

"Bloody hell, we had a dodgy caretaker and a groundsman, and that was it."

"Different times, boss."

"Indeed. Well, good."

"We haven't been able to contact the ex-head. We have his address and we sent a patrol round but there was no response to their call, and we haven't been able to reach him on the phone. We've left messages and are contacting next of kin. He has a son who lives in London and a brother in Yorkshire."

"Right. Keep on trying with the headmaster. A word in my office if you would, DC Lewis."

"DCI Scunthorpe needs to view the film of Sue's accident. Arrange it, will you? Quick as you can. I know it's important but finding this bloke before he causes any more trouble takes precedence, in my opinion. Sue is dead, it's awful and we need to be sure we know what happened, but I don't want any more death."

"You're convinced, aren't you?"

"Convinced Stewart is our killer? Yes, yes, I am. Do you have doubts?"

"I always have doubts, boss. Unless the killer is standing over the body with a bloody knife and a signed confession, I always have doubts."

"Yes, I know you're right, but my gut tells me this bloke is who we are looking for. Now, I'm going to go through my messages. I anticipate a call from DCI Scunthorpe after he's seen the CCTV footage, but I need to be told at once if we find this ex-headmaster Mr Park. If we don't have contact in the next hour – I want us up there. Where is it?"

"Near Binsey."

"Okay, alert Dan and Paul. I'll want to leave you here to hold things together."

"Are you thinking the headmaster is in trouble?"

"I think he could be, and I need to go and see. Once I've spoken to the DCI about the issue of Sue's accident."

"What about her?"

Neither of them had heard Brian Finch come into the room. They didn't know how long he had been there or how much he had heard.

"Brian. I was in with Bob Scunthorpe earlier. The way the conversation played out I didn't have any choice but to put him in the picture. I had to tell him about my suspicion there was someone on the scaffolding."

She saw his face darken with anger.

"Got in first, did you? Did you tell him I'd spent hours going over all the footage? Did you tell him I'd been up half the night finalising my report to ensure it was full and complete? Did you tell him, as well as all that, I had spotted your suspect with the knife?"

"I filled him in on what we were thinking."

Finch turned on his heel and stomped out of the office.

"Thank you, DI Miller. Thank you very much," he shouted as he disappeared down the corridor.

Kate watched him go and then turned back, her face screwed into an 'Oh dear' expression. "Don't think he's happy."

"Nope. Don't think he is."

"On that note, boss, I wanted to make a suggestion."

"Right. Carry on, unless it's something to do with DI Finch's man bits."

"Erm, no – it's not." Kate struggled to keep her face straight. "No, if you're right then maybe we should bring in a lip reader."

"Oh right. I wonder if we have a clear enough view of her face?"

"I think it must be worth a try."

"Get onto it, will you? I'll ring Bob Scunthorpe. Mention DI Finch might be heading over there and tell him your suggestion. Perhaps if I speak to him now, I can convince him to let me get out and head up to the ex-head's place. There's no reported sighting of the van, is there?"

"No. I would have mentioned it, boss."

"Yes. 'course you would."

Chapter 55

Tanya picked up the phone. She knew what she was about to do could be regarded as an attempt to cover her arse and keep Finch off her back. But she needed to get out of the office as quickly as possible. DCI Scunthorpe's secretary connected her.

"Sir. I had the CCTV footage sent over."

"Yes. I am viewing it now."

"Okay. DI Finch is on his way over to you. He has viewed all the film much more thoroughly than I have. It was his research into the incident that lead to us finding the murder weapon in my case. I believe he has spent a lot of time writing up a fully considered report."

"Right. Thank you, Tanya. I look forward to discussing this with him. I believe I hear him in the outer office now. I appreciate your call, good of you to make sure there is credit whcre it's due. In the circumstances I think you can carry on. No need for me to take up your time."

"There is just one thing. DC Lewis has suggested the services of a lip reader. If we can have an idea of what was being said, I think it will be very useful."

"Absolutely. When I speak to DI Finch, I'll mention it."

"I have taken the liberty of having DC Lewis get the ball rolling on that."

"Well done. I'll speak to you later. Tanya, take care."

"Yes sir. Thank you, sir."

Had she dropped him right in it? Had he even thought of a lip reader? Was his report as thorough as she had insinuated? Well, if he had done a good job, he would have no problem. If he hadn't and couldn't answer the question the DCI was going to ask, so be it. She turned off her computer, picked up her bag and went to meet Price and Harris in the car park.

* * *

It wasn't a long drive out towards the tiny village of Binsey. They took the route through Summertown. In the summer it would have been very pretty. Today the cloud was heavy and there was cold drizzle in the air. The roads were slick and as they pulled onto the grass verge outside the white detached house the tyres squelched in mud.

It was quiet. They heard a rooster somewhere complaining about the weather. A dog barked but there was the shut down feel of a dreary day. They knocked on the door, peered through the windows and the rickety door of an outbuilding. They could find no sign of anyone.

"Try the other houses," Tanya said. She pulled up the hood on her jacket and walked towards the tiny white cottage next door. There was a wall, old stone, weathered but well maintained. The gate was open. Beyond was a small, dripping woodland. Not much more than a large garden but full of established trees, oaks and sycamores. There was no way to tell which property it belonged to but there was an open barn across the back of a small area of yard. She glanced back to the road. Paul and Dan were still visible. Dan was talking to a woman in the doorway of a house in the other direction. She asked him inside, Tanya watched as he wiped his feet on the mat and vanished through the door. Paul was crossing towards the village pub. She grinned; he was drawn towards it even though there was no chance of a drink.

She splashed through the puddles. Stopped and considered going back for her boots but she was almost there now, and her shoes were already wet and muddy. From the road, the building had looked a bit dilapidated but now she was closer she could see it was sound and taken care of. There was a long wooden table inside and an oil drum barbecue pushed up against the half-timbered wall. Sacks and folding chairs were piled into the corners. She called out but there was no response. A narrow path led to the corner. The bushes needed pruning and by the time she had made it down the side her coat was soaked, and her feet were wet and cold.

She turned in a slow circle. At the rear was a patch of grass and then the trees. She guessed that this area was part of the headmaster's property. It was quiet and gloomy and for a moment the isolation felt freaky. She liked her house in the middle of a street. She liked the feel of other people around her, the noise of traffic, even at night. Streetlights, children shouting. This was too quiet. It was time to go back and admit to the others the trip had been a waste of time. They still needed to trace the ex-head, but he wasn't home. On the upside, if they couldn't find him, probably Stewart Dawes couldn't either.

She turned to make her way back through the overgrown shrubbery. Looked down at her coat, the smears of dirt across the sleeve. She'd have to have the thing cleaned and pride wouldn't let her claim the cost on expenses. She couldn't afford it though, not right now. She brushed at the muck. That made it worse. She could sponge it but didn't want to get grubbier. The other way made more sense. There was a small patch of muddy ground and then the hard surface of the driveway. She cursed under her breath, she could have accessed the yard by there and saved her shoes and coat.

She hadn't noticed the tyre tracks from where she had been standing. The grass wasn't torn up but where the house drive met the garden there was a small flower bed. It was empty, waiting for planting in a few weeks but now, the soil was disturbed, mud on the grass. There was no reason for someone to drive a vehicle this way. There was the drive, the yard, the road, all more suitable for parking. She followed the marks of wheels to where they vanished into the trees. Why would anyone take a car in there? She was sure it was a car; a garden vehicle wouldn't make these tracks and there wasn't room for a tractor.

She pulled out her phone. They needed to go into the woods, find whatever had been driven this way. She felt a quiver of excitement, heard the crunch of feet on the path.

She called out, "Dan, is that you?"

Chapter 56

Bob Scunthorpe was going to be furious with her. After the nausea and the pain and the confusion, that was what she thought. The lump on her head was throbbing, her hair was clumpy and wet, she could feel the trickle of blood down the side of her face and round her ear. She had realised quickly what had happened.

She felt the rattle, the rumble of the engine and the sickening jerk and bump of the van. She had been confused for a minute because where she was laying was soft, not a hard floor. She turned her aching head carefully and saw bags lined against the panels, a couple of plastic crates, a pile of folded blankets. She moved and the tarpaulin covering the narrow mattress under her crackled. She froze. From where she was, she could see the back of his head and his shoulders. There was the other thing as well. The bundle, long and narrow, wrapped in black plastic and tied with blue nylon string. It was laid across the vehicle behind the seats. The knees, she knew they were knees, were bent to make it fit. She knew what it was.

Her arms were tied behind her back, numb and useless. Her ankles were tied, not tightly. She didn't think he had expected her to regain consciousness so quickly. She couldn't shuffle, the tarpaulin made too much noise. Keeping movement minimal, Tanya looked around. Her shoulder bag wasn't there. She wondered where her phone was. He might have it. It had been in the garden. She had seen the tyre tracks. She had been going to call the others. Maybe she lost her phone, maybe he had it. If he had it, they could trace it. She hoped he had it. Bob Scunthorpe was going to be furious. Her eyes clouded with tears and she blinked them away. It was just reaction. There was no point in crying. It wasn't going to help.

The van didn't have side windows. From where she was lying, she could see through the upper part of the windscreen beyond the dark bulk of the seat backs. It was raining, the wipers swept back and forth. The radio was on the news. She tilted her head backwards, twisting her neck, slowly, quietly. Through the windows in the rear door she could see trees, clouds, no buildings. Okay so they weren't back in the city. It didn't matter but it was information.

The lads would know by now that she was in trouble. They had been nearby. They might even have heard the van's engine through the trees. But she didn't know how far away it had been, she didn't remember being dragged or carried. They must know by now and they would have raised the alarm. They had the registration. As soon as he drove on a main road, he'd be picked up by the ANPR cameras. All she had to do was lie here, keep quiet and wait for him to show himself.

She looked back again – still trees, clouds. *Come on, get on the main road, you bastard.*

It didn't happen, in fact the drive wasn't very long. Tanya saw the glow from streetlamps and hope sprung but it was short and swiftly passed. She closed her eyes, tried to visualise the map. Beyond Binsey there was Wytham, Godstow, Wolvercote, no not Wolvercote, there were houses there, streetlights. She needed to concentrate. She didn't know what time it was, not accurately, but the light in the sky, such as there was, was brighter out of the rear windows, so, they were heading east. What was east? Kidlington, Deddington, on to Banbury. It was important to know where she was. If she had the chance, she would need to let her people know where she was. If she was able to run, she needed to have an idea where she was running to. She simply needed to place herself, to know where she was. Duke's Cut was this way, the lake where bodies were found. Woodland, water, ponds, and ditches. Her stomach turned. She felt sick. That wasn't happening. She would not end her life in a ditch in the middle of the country. She would not.

He turned the van sharply and the tree cover was denser now. The ride was bumpier. Okay, off road. More information. Then the sound of gravel spitting from beneath the wheels, and he stopped.

He clambered out and slammed the door, the crunch and scrape of shoes on hard ground. Tanya closed her eyes, she needed him to think she was still unconscious. She forced her muscles to soften and relax; her breathing to slow. It was hard and she was scared. She had been scared before, it was okay, it meant the buzz of adrenaline. She would use it when the bastard came to her. She waited; he didn't come. All was quiet, there were birds.

Now he was gone she shuffled and twisted – if she could get the ties loose then she could take him, of course she could. She tensed her legs, tried to pull her ankles apart, each time the binds were looser. He was crap at tying someone up. Plonker. She strained and tensed, strained and tensed. Now they were loose enough for her to move her feet, she wedged the toe of her right foot under the heel of her left and levered off her shoe, thank God she hadn't gone back for the boots. Now the other shoe and soon her feet were free. She pushed and wriggled, hips, legs, shoulders until she was against the side of the van and then upright. Okay, that was better, upright was good. Now she had to get her arms free. This was okay, he was an idiot and she was going to take him down.

She shuffled to where there was a hook to secure a luggage strap. No problem, all she needed to do now was hook the ties over and she would be loose.

She had been panting with the effort, the tarp scrunching and crackling; she hadn't heard him coming, not until the rattle of the handle on the back door of the van.

Chapter 57

Tanya threw herself across the mattress, assuming a position as near as possible to the one she had been in when she regained her senses. She bent her knees and held her feet together, one on top of the other. The back door of the van opened. Slowly. She smelled the rain-drenched air, sodden woodland and just a faint residue of diesel fumes from the cooling engine.

Stewart Dawes reached in and pulled a spade from beneath the cargo floor. He hopped onto the bumper and leaned towards her, poking and prodding. She held herself still. He grunted and jumped back to the ground. She decided he was an idiot. She could sort out an idiot.

Shuffling and rolling she turned in the narrow space until she could shuffle across the tarp towards the rear door. When he came back, she'd be ready for him. Better if her hands were free. He'd tied them with something hard and narrow – it would be cable ties, wouldn't it? That would be a problem. The bloody things were tough. She could feel them even now digging into the flesh of her wrists. Without a blade she wouldn't be able to move them.

Okay. Her feet were free. Her head was pounding but she wasn't dizzy now. So, no concussion. That was a welcome thought.

She stretched upwards to peer through the little square windows in the van doors. She couldn't see Dawes. All there was from her restricted view were trees, sky, and rain clouds.

The lads would have pulled out all the stops by now. They would be looking for her. Shouldn't take them long. DCI Scunthorpe was going to be livid, especially if they had put the helicopter up. It would play hell with his budget. Still, she hoped they had. The car would be visible, hot engine making it glow like a neon light. He would be visible. He had taken a spade, it made sense he'd be digging. A bloke digging was going to glow like one of those kids in that silly old advert about Windscale. She giggled. Okay, that wasn't good. This wasn't a time for giggling. She had to keep control. She tried again to move her hands. That pushed away any hysterical amusement. Christ, it hurt. She knew there was bleeding. It was foul, slipping under the plastic, running down her fingers.

There was the clank now of the spade, she could hear it. He must have hit a different layer in the ground. It was obvious what he was doing. The poor sod in the front – it had to be the ex-headmaster – was going in a shallow grave. Well, not if she could help it.

Kneeling or sitting, which was going to give her the most force? She would have one shot at this. Kneeling, she could propel herself forward like a spring. She wriggled her legs underneath her and sat on her feet. No, that was no good. Her feet hurt and there was no way to know just how long it would be. Her legs would be useless quickly. So, maybe sitting was a workable option. Sitting with her knees bent, her feet flat. No good.

She had to stand.

The van wasn't spacious enough for her to stand straight, she wasn't tall, not quite one metre seventy so she didn't know how Steward Dawes coped, living in it. Then again, she didn't care, and he wouldn't be living in it again. Not after today.

Standing, scrunched over, her head lowered, shoulders hunched, was far from comfortable. She bent her knees, rolled her head from side to side and flexed her shoulders. She couldn't sit again because there was no way to guess how long he would be.

It was almost dark and through the window she saw the occasional flash of light, a torch, the light bouncing off the trees as he moved around. Yes, good, she would see him coming. Yes, he was an idiot. No competition for her at all.

The rain had eased a bit and the sound of digging ceased. Now, she had to be ready, she flexed and tensed. The torch light moved nearer. Her stomach clenched, she swallowed, took a deep breath, waited.

A beam of light flashed across the little square windows. His feet crunched over the stony ground. She waited for the rattle of the van doors, poised to throw herself at him, all the force of her body behind her.

The windows darkened and his footsteps moved on.

She listened, ears on high alert. She hadn't prepared for this. She should have thought of it. She heard him throw down the spade, walk the length of the vehicle. The light flashed across the windscreen. The quiet click as he pulled down the handle and then a small noise as he pulled open the front door.

She threw herself to the mattress, rolled onto her side, closed her eyes but she knew it was too late. He must have seen her, heard her, sensed her. He had to know she was awake. She held her breath, screwed her eyes closed and cursed herself for not planning for this. Who was the idiot now?

Chapter 58

"She's a loose cannon. Unreliable. I've said it before. This is not the first time, far from it. There are regulations, properly researched routines to protect everyone. It's as if she's never done any training." Brian Finch paced back and forth in the incident room, ranting.

Kate had her landline phone wedged between her shoulder and her chin. Her mobile began to vibrate across the desk as she typed rapidly into her laptop. One of the uniformed constables, who had been about to go off duty until the call went out, printed images of Binsey from Google Earth. She pinned one on the whiteboard alongside a picture of the large white house where Mr Park lived.

In Summertown, the scream of sirens attracted attention. As the blue and white cars and the crew carriers sped through the district, the public tutted and made assumptions and went back to their own lives. In Binsey the neighbours were out in force. There weren't many of them and they all knew Mr Park. They pushed through the bushes, peered into barns and sheds, and some had gone all the way to the riverbank where they stepped along in boots and waders and scanned the water. They all wanted to be the hero who found the headmaster and the missing police officer. None of them wanted to be the one who came across the gory remains of either.

Dan had driven off in Tanya's car. He had the address of Stewart Dawes's brother programmed into her sat nav. He ignored the speed limits, screaming across junctions with his horn blaring and the integrated blue lights illuminating the gathering dark.

When he opened the door to find a warrant card brandished in his face, Tony Dawes sighed and stepped back. "I knew this wasn't going to go away. What has he done now? I told your colleague already I don't know what he's up to. I don't see him often. I'm sorry but in this case, I am not my brother's keeper."

"This is very urgent, Mr Dawes. We reckon your brother may be in serious trouble. We need to find him quickly. We've been unable to locate him using technology. And believe me we've tried. We need any hint, any idea at all where he may be. We've got a helicopter on standby. We've got a large number of officers searching but we need your help. Please. Is there anywhere you can think of that he might be? Somewhere he would choose to hide?"

"Hide? What the hell is it you think he might have done? I mean, he's a bit of a prat sometimes and a narky bugger but–" He stopped. "God, shit just got real, didn't it?"

"I'm afraid you could be right there. Please think. Where would he go if he was in trouble?"

"No." Tony shook his head. "Well, what I mean is – I don't know. He's been away for years. He wanders about, he hasn't got a settled address."

Dan clenched his fists, pursed his lips together. "Okay. Back in the day, when he did live here. What about where your parents used to live?"

"Well, yes, that was in Summertown."

"I need the address."

Once he had the number and the street name, Dan rang Kate who despatched a couple of cars to the area.

"Anywhere else, Mr Dawes? Grandparents' houses?"

"No, they've been dead a long time. We didn't really know them."

"What about around Binsey? Is there anywhere near there he knew well? Please think. This could quite literally be a matter of life and death."

"Shit. No, erm – let me think. Binsey. That's in the sticks, by the river."

"Yes. Yes, we know where it is. Did Stewart know the area?"

"Well of course. It's not that far from Summertown. We used to go that way on our bikes but like I say it's years ago."

There was a short silence filled with Dan Price's rapid breathing. He paced to the window to glance outside, then back into the living room. This was taking them nowhere. He rubbed a hand over his face. "Anything, Tony?"

"Well, there was a place. Up on the way to Swinford, cross country. There are some woods there. We used to go that way. Camped a couple of times in a stupid little tent. Got wet through. I hated it. He didn't though. I think he liked it there. He used to go on his own. After the trouble at the school he camped for a couple of weeks, on his own."

"Where? Exactly where?"

"Oh, erm on the way to Swinford as I say, across the river and the bypass. There was a pub, The White Hart and then out the back are fields and woods. It probably belonged to someone, but we never got into trouble. I suppose he could be there."

Dan spun away, called on his phone. "Kate. Area of woodland between Wytham and Swinford. Camped there as a child. I'm on my way but we need the chopper up. We can't just go careering wildly through the trees. There's nothing at Binsey, is there?"

"No. Tyre tracks leaving the wooded area near the house and then nothing. We've got plenty of people on the ground, but it's gone nowhere. Nobody saw anything, the rain had everyone inside. I'll get on to Bob Scunthorpe right away."

"I'll do that." Brian Finch grabbed his jacket and stormed from the room.

Kate Lewis said nothing, she raised her eyes at the spare constable who shook her head. No words were needed.

Chapter 59

Tanya knew he'd seen her standing in the back of the van. As he ran down the side of it to the rear, wrenching open the double doors, there was no point in pretending any more, it was time to fight.

Stepping up onto the bumper he leaned in, reaching for her legs as she shuffled away from him on the mattress. She rolled and wriggled as he came further and further inside. She had scuttled around with her feet towards him. Now she was tensing and pushing herself backwards with her heels, drawing him towards her, bringing him into the small space to reduce the odds.

She felt the bulk stop her. She heard the crackle of plastic as the bag shifted in the narrow space between the seat backs and the end of the mattress. She couldn't think about that now, couldn't let thoughts of the poor dead teacher interfere with what she had to do. She leaned backwards against the bundled body and drew her knees up close. As Dawes crawled forwards, she tensed. Ready. Coiled. There would be one moment, just one probably when she would have the chance to put all of her strength behind the thrust, and if she missed, he would be on top of her. With her hands bound and nowhere to go, it would be over.

He was puffing now along the space, on all fours in the dim interior. She held back; knees bent, braced against the foul bundle of the headmaster's remains. Waiting. Dawes stopped, he understood the danger he had put himself in and he growled, fury and frustration narrowing his eyes. He reached for Tanya's foot, she pulled it back away. She couldn't shuffle forwards, he had to come for her, nearer, just a little bit nearer.

"Come on you, arse, come and get me. If you dare. Let's see how brave you are now. No knife, no little old woman. Come on."

"Shut up," he hissed. "Just shut up. Why can't you leave me alone? I've got a job to do, why can't you leave me alone? You and your stupid mate. You should have gone away. No need to come asking questions. I've waited years for this, years of wasted time, they spoiled my life, all of them and now it's my turn. All of them, in their big houses, with their nice lives, their fancy cars. Families, money and they stole my chance."

"Oh, come on. Mrs Barker, a nice life. She was a poor lonely old widow. What harm could she do you?"

"She'd had it all. Years and years of it while I lived in squats and slums and cleaned toilets and swept floors. Even now she offered me money. '*Here, take this, take the money hidden upstairs.*' There it was in her airing cupboard, bundles of cash hidden away. Oh, I took it, yes, I took it, mine by right that was. I could have been someone, I could have had all they had. Now it's happening again. You and your mate. Asking questions, poking your noses in. Well, I got rid of her and now it's your turn."

"My mate?"

"Yes, that nosy bitch. Coming down to the site, stirring things up. Trying to lose me my job. '*Come down please. Come down I need to speak with you.*'" He affected a high-pitched squeak as he spoke and Tanya saw, of course, the accident. Sue.

"That was you? But she didn't know. We didn't know."

"Well, duh. Of course, it was me. The stupid little bitch. Did she really think I was going to let her spoil everything? Again. Again, and again, and again. People interfering, offering advice, trying to *understand*." As he spoke, he thumped at the mattress, his eyes were wet, and spittle flew from his mouth. That was good, he was out of control, it was good. She had to draw him closer.

"So, you threw down the scaffolding boards, you killed my friend. But you can't get me, you really can't. They're coming for you. It's all over. My team, they're on their way right now."

"No, no, no. They don't know where we are. Nobody knows. Nobody comes here. This is my place. This has always been my place. All the time abroad, this was where I thought of. My place in the woods. Nobody is coming here."

"They'll trace my phone."

He laughed and shook his head. "Ha, you think I'm stupid. I ditched that way back. No, they'll never find you. I was putting him in. I'd got everything ready."

He pointed beyond her to the black-wrapped corpse. "It was a mistake with missus bloody Barker. I had to leave her. Those stupid boys, banging the fence. Climbing up. But not this time, they'll never find him. And it's okay, I've made the hole bigger. Plenty of room for both of you."

"You'll have to get me first." Tense, coiled, ready, she waited. One more arm's length, that's all it needed. *Come on, you bastard.*

And then it was over, he reached for her, stretched and unbalanced on his knees. Tanya drew back her legs and thrust her feet at him, no holding back, all the power she had behind it. Straight for his face, both feet and again and again, his shoulders now as he tried to turn away. She was grunting, panting, and kicking, over and over. It would have been so much better with her shoes on, but you work with what you've got. She felt his nose break, saw the spatter of blood as he shook his head. She kicked out again. She was lying flat now on her back, her legs pumping one after the other and he rolled and shuffled back, groaning and spitting, away from the constant thunder of her feet on his face, head, body. She heard screaming, realised it was her own voice and stopped.

He slid from the open doorway onto the forest floor and then crabbed away, his hands wiping at his ruined face. As she rolled to the back of the van, she saw him stagger to his feet and shake his head and then reach over to where he had leaned the spade against the trunk of a tree. He grabbed it low down on the handle, turned and stepped back, unsteady, sobbing but armed now, coming to where she lay, wrists bound and bleeding, on her belly on the mattress in the van.

She saw him smile, the blood-stained teeth a dull glow in the gathering dusk.

Chapter 60

The thunder came from nowhere. One minute it wasn't there – just the swish of wind in the trees, the sound of her breathing fast and noisy, Dawes' feet on the ground as he moved back towards her, brandishing the spade.

Tanya had slid to the open van doors. Her legs dangled over the edge. She was unsteady and awkward with her hands still tied behind her, but she was going to run. No way was she sitting here waiting for him and his bloody spade. She dropped and rolled and that was when they heard the thunder of the helicopter coming through the trees. He stopped. Peered upwards, and turned. It was all the chance she needed to slide upwards, braced against the rear corner of the vehicle.

Louder it came and louder, now they could feel it, thrumming in the air. She didn't wait, didn't look back just lit out into the undergrowth. It was hellish, branches and twigs whipping at her face, vines grabbing at her feet. She knew it was an impossible task to get away but at least she would have tried. She stumbled and fell, rolled, and pushed herself up on the trunk of an oak. He had paused to look for the source of the noise, unsure of which way to run, but he was coming. She heard him thrashing after her.

The thrum of the rotor blades pounded the air, the trees were bending now, leaves shuttering down around her and the light, the brilliant cone of the searchlight sweeping through the darkness.

Then came the loudspeaker – "Stewart Dawes, put down your weapon. You can't get away. Step into the clearing, throw down the weapon and lay on the ground."

It was loud, it was scary, but it didn't stop him. He was out of control, panicked, and she was his quarry. She pushed on, through the undergrowth, sobbing and gasping, but still moving forwards.

He was under the canopy now, hidden by the woods. She heard the helicopter wheel and turn, she saw the light circling, but he still came after her, carrying the spade, hacking at the trees as he passed.

Tanya tripped on a vine snaking across the floor. She landed on her knees and cried out with the jolt of pain. She tucked and rolled but the surface was sharp and unforgiving; she was exhausted and there was no strength left to drag herself across the wet ground to a place where she could push her body upwards. He was coming now, and it would soon be over. They would catch him though and that was some comfort. There would be justice for Mrs Barker, the headmaster and the pregnant woman a world away.

She turned to look at him as he burst through the trees. He was bloodied and battered but he was standing, and he was armed. She closed her eyes.

The light from the chopper burned through her lids, the loudspeaker roared in the air, she heard the crackle of branches and the scream of rage and she braced for the end.

"You bastard. You evil bastard. No bloody way! Hang on, boss. I'm here. Hang on."

She opened her eyes and there he was: Dan Price with a great tree limb in his hands and his face contorted with rage.

He hit Dawes hard, it would later be confirmed he had fractured his skull. The man slumped to the ground just a couple of metres from where Tanya knelt, sobbing and shaking. The helicopter was circling, there were blue lights in the sky and in the trees and the sound of sirens and running feet. Dan Price placed the lump of wood carefully to one side. "I expect we'll have to turn that in," he said. He tried for jocular, but his voice was quivery and when he leaned to help her to her feet, Tanya saw his hands were trembling. "Shit, boss. That was close. Too bloody close."

She wanted to answer him, wanted to thank him, make some sort of smart comment of her own but it was almost beyond her. It took all her strength to breathe and not to let herself fall into the welcome dark that was trying to take her away. She pulled herself together as much as she could. Nodded towards Dan's head. "You've made a mess of your hair, Dan."

He grinned and rubbed a hand over the bedraggled mop on top of his head. "I was going for something more casual."

Tanya smiled back at him. He blushed.

The woods filled quickly with bodies, noise, and rush. She heard someone calling for an ambulance. Dawes was groaning and they were talking with him, keeping him still, reassuring him he was going to be okay. They had to do it, they weren't demented killers, they were public servants and it had to be done according to the rules. But she would make the arrest, it was her collar. Dan had cut the plastic ties with his penknife. She forced herself upright, walked as steadily as she could across the tiny clearing and said the words. "Stewart Dawes, I am arresting you on suspicion of the murder of…" She paused, looked at Dan and took a breath. "I am arresting you on suspicion of the murder of Carol Barker…" They would have him for Sue's death, she was sure of it and he would suffer for that, but for the sake of the poor lonely widow who bled out under another tree, her name should be spoken now.

Chapter 61

Although it had been delayed, the funeral they held for Sue was a good event. Her mother had decided that, especially as she had been killed in the line of duty, her daughter deserved all the pomp and ceremony she was entitled to. The team were pallbearers, in uniform, sombre and smart. Kate managed to keep the tears away until after the coffin was placed on the catafalque and although there was sobbing and sniffles the family held themselves together. There was a heart-breaking picture of the young woman in the front of the chapel and the evening news carried a report of the hero policewoman.

Knowing Sue had been killed by an enraged murderer intent on escape rather than by accident had eased Tanya's conscience a little, but she knew she would always have residual doubt. If she hadn't been irritated by the young woman's lack of commitment, lack of a serious approach to her work, then maybe she wouldn't have sent her to her death that day. She kept the thoughts to herself as she spoke to Mrs Bakshi and the devastated brothers.

Afterwards there was the get-together in the pub. It was a foregone conclusion; it wouldn't have seemed right not to. There were toasts and memories and black humour and all the things that helped to get them through.

Kate slid into the seat beside Tanya. "Good result all round, boss. I reckon Sue would have been pleased."

"No, she wouldn't," Tanya said.

"No, probably not. Well, anyway it feels better than a stupid mishap."

"I guess," Tanya answered.

"Well, the rest of it though. That bugger going behind bars for a long time. It's good, yeah. And Mrs Barker's daughter – a healthy baby boy. That was nice."

"It was and it was good of them to let us know."

"You did get justice for their mum, after all."

"It was a mess though, and think of the headmaster. If I'd have caught on sooner, he'd still be alive now. Poor old bloke."

"I know, boss, but you did good and you saved the others. He was intending harm to all the people involved. Are you okay now? Injuries all healed?"

"Oh yes, actually there wasn't much. My arms were a bit knackered for a while but really in the end nothing to speak of." Tanya flexed her wrists as she spoke.

"Did you do anything interesting while you were on sick?"

"No, not really. I went up to see my sister in Edinburgh." Tanya wasn't about to share details of the arguments she had with Fiona, the rows about her money mismanagement and the loan that, though it got the bank off her back, now made her beholden to her family in a way that she had never wanted.

"Dan Price is still swaggering around. Tells everyone who'll listen about the major rescue."

"I can't begrudge him that. Seeing him come roaring through the trees with that bloody great tree branch is something I don't think I'll ever forget. Honestly, though, he really did save me. A few more minutes and I reckon

I'd have been a goner. I'm glad he's getting a commendation, he deserves it. I'll come back for that."

"How do you mean, come back?"

Tanya turned now to look Kate in the eye. "I've asked for a transfer."

"What? No. Where to?"

"I've asked to go to Birmingham. It's still near enough for me to commute, so I can keep the house."

"But, well – bloody hell, Birmingham. Why?"

I just feel that it's time for me to have a change. I like the people we've met up there. I liked the different vibe, the bigger city. I thought I'd try it for a while, see how it works out."

"Well, good luck. I suppose you might as well give it a go now, while you're still young." Kate took a swig of her red wine.

"I want to try something different. It'll do me good anyway, a change of scene. It's a different thing up there. Big city crime. I need a change. It's only twelve months and then I'll probably be back."

"I'll miss you, boss. The team will miss you, but if it's what you have to do – good luck to you."

They hugged. Tanya was taken aback by the tears springing to her eyes. Hugging? Crying? Oh yes, it was well past time for a change of scene. At the end of the day the secondment would include extra expenses and she could pay Fiona back much more quickly.

"Right, my round, you lot," she said and grinned at the jeering and the cheering. She would miss the team and that surprised her more than anything.

The End

List of characters

The Team:

Robert (Bob) Scunthorpe – Detective Chief Inspector

Late fifties. Decent and honourable senior officer. Married. One son.

Tanya Miller – Detective Inspector

Early thirties. Younger daughter in the family with one sibling. Always in the shadow of her brilliant older sister as they grew up. A shopaholic, she returned to Oxford from a previous posting and at first worked in the missing persons section until moving to the serious crimes team.

Sue Rollinson (Suhita Rollinson-Bakshi) – Detective Constable

Young, unmarried, from a largish mixed-race family; father dead, mother an estate agent. Three brothers, one sister.

Paul Harris – Detective Sergeant

A plodder. Recently married and a bit of a bloke. Doesn't really get the whole PC thing. Lives in a rental flat with his wife Nicole.

Kate Lewis – Detective Constable

Fifties, heading for retirement. Content with her life and achievements but refuses to be side-lined due to her age and lack of professional progression. Happily married with three teenage daughters. Skilled with the computer and a good organiser.

Dan Price – Detective Constable

Young and insecure. Quiet and keeps his head down. Partly because he was bullied when he was younger but also because he isn't sure how widely known it is that he is gay. Recently started living with Gary, an airline Pilot. Gary has a large flat and plenty of money but there are tensions because Dan's shifts and Gary's travels mean they don't see each other, leaving Dan living alone in what feels like someone else's house.

Charlie Lambert – Detective Inspector

Recently moved to Merseyside. Married to Carol. They have one baby – Joshua – who he dotes on. He is a family man from a large Jamaican family.

Brian Finch – Detective Inspector

Relatively new to the team. Tall, good-looking, computer savvy and connected via an uncle to the top brass. Arrogant and driven.

Others:

Simon Hewitt – medical examiner

Tall, good-looking, dark brown hair and grey eyes, late forties, unmarried.

Moira – morgue receptionist

Late thirties and dedicated to 'protecting' the morgue staff from hassle. Abrupt and unfriendly but tolerated by the morgue staff as she runs the place so efficiently.

Mrs Green – Tanya's cleaner

DCI Parker – Birmingham, Snow Hill – Liaison

Tony Marsh – civilian despatcher

Dave Chance – Senior Crime Scene Investigator

Fifties. Grey and grizzled. Dry sense of humour.

Theresa Hunt – Detective Sergeant

Terry – Snow Hill custody sergeant

Carol Barker – ex-schoolteacher

Late fifties. Daughter in Australia. Husband dead.

Elaine Cartwright – next-door neighbour to the victim, married to Dave.

Stella Barker – Carol's daughter
Pregnant. Married to Ollie.

Jayden Gormon – caught up in county lines drug problem.

Lydie Gormon – Jayden's mother. Divorced. A nurse.

Carl Grant – caught up in the county lines drug problem.

Kayleigh Grant – Carl's sister. Thirteen but precocious.

Frances Grant – Carl's mother.

Tracey – Kayleigh's friend.

Gregor Belic – Serbian drug dealer and people trafficker.

Ruthless and lacking any compassion.

George Roberts and Stewart Dawes – contractors

If you enjoyed this book, please let others know by leaving a quick review on Amazon. Also, if you spot anything untoward in the paperback, get in touch. We strive for the best quality and appreciate reader feedback.

editor@thebookfolks.com

www.thebookfolks.com

Also available in this series:

BROKEN ANGEL
BURNING GREED
BRUTAL PURSUIT
BRAZEN ESCAPE

Other books by Diane Dickson:

TWIST OF TRUTH
TANGLED TRUTH
BONE BABY
LEAVING GEORGE
WHO FOLLOWS
THE GRAVE
PICTURES OF YOU
LAYERS OF LIES
DEPTHS OF DECEPTION
YOU'RE DEAD
SINGLE TO EDINBURGH